Splendid Shore

D0869756

LINDA THORNDIKE

PAGE PUBLISHING, INC.
Conneaut Lake, PA

First originally published by Page Publishing 2020

ISBN 978-1-64628-268-5 (pbk)
ISBN 978-1-64701-571-8 (hc)
ISBN 978-1-64628-269-2 (digital)

Printed in the United States of America

To my husband, Steven Dingman, who maintained a sense of humor through twelve years of my writing *Splendid Shore*

PART 1

Rolling Ripples

CHAPTER 1

Lady of the Lake

June 1956, Cynthia and Hardy

"Oh, Hardy, it's such a pretty stone, but I don't like my present. I want a green one," fiery five-year-old Cynthia Parkton told her four-year-old cousin Harden Alden. She pressed her lips together in a firm pout.

At the edge of the woods, adorned in her Aunt Natty's silk scarves, Cynthia elevated herself on branches in the center of the leaf castle she and Hardy built to play Lady of The Lake, the imaginary game they created together.

"I have to spank you now," she proclaimed, patiently tilting up her regal head toward him.

"I know, I know. Then I will find you a pretty green rock," Hardy babbled back to her.

The summer sun glistened off his dense black-rimmed glasses. Other than the glasses, little Hardy stood stark naked. Then he squatted on the ground before his cousin with his bared buttocks exposed to her. With scarves flowing about her, nymphlike Cynthia plucked a branch with leaves to spank him. In shameless suspense, he waited on all fours. Then the explosion of her unruly strikes yielded him to her command. The whacks left his exposed bottom aglow, red-hot.

After the spanking, naked as a jaybird with his little penis bobbing, he scrambled to his feet. Then he scurried into the woods to find an emerald-colored treasure for his princess Cynthia, The Lady of The Lake. In their fanciful game, she made it his duty to please her with treasures.

"Why don't I ever get to be The Lady of The Lake?" he complained when he returned to Cynthia with a new emerald treasure for her hoard.

"Because I'm beautiful and a princess, Hardy. Only I can command and punish kings and princes. Put your swimming suit back on. We better go back home to The Lodge. Our mommies might be back now looking for us."

Tenderly holding hands, the two cousins scampered back to The Lodge. Hardy's young flesh still stung under his swimming suit, but he did not complain.

At The Lodge, Hardy's mother saw them first but had not missed them yet.

"Isn't it just delightful how cute you two play together," she said. Hardy's mother beamed down at them with an approving nod of her head. "And you, Cynthia, how beautiful you look dressed up in Natty's colored silk sheer scarves. The pretty green and blue ones draped on you make you look like a little princess."

"Thank you," Cynthia answered politely with a pretend smile. She already knew that.

The Legend Goes Like This

"Daddy, tell me the story again," Cynthia begged at bedtime.

"Okay, okay, sure, honey, I will." Put Put Parkton sat down on the side of his daughter's bed. "In the bottomless green depths of The Lake lives the beauteous, radiant Great Lady Water Spirit who owns all The Lake," he began. "You can't go out on The Lake without her permission. She'll be angry if you don't worship her on the shore first, and bring a gift out of your provisions. If you anger her, she'll come up from her deep emerald home when you're far out on the water.

She'll make a mighty whirlpool and turn the pure green-colored water into a solid rock of jade. You'll be dragged down under it, never to be seen again." He made a swooping circular motion with his arm. "All the Winnebago Indians came at least once in a lifetime to worship the Great Lady Water Spirit living under *Daycholah*, honey."

"I know the Winnebago word *Daycholah* means waters of deep green color, Daddy. And I know about all the little Indian trails that led to Daycholah for them to bring presents to the pretty princess under the water. The Indian word *Monapacataca* means the home we love so much, doesn't it, Daddy?" She sighed. Her eyes began to close.

"Yes, yes, it does. What a big word for you to always remember," he said softly. He pulled up the summer sheets and lightly tucked her. "Sleep time now, Cynthia." She fell asleep to dream of the green jewels Hardy found for her today.

Spring 1964, Cynthia

At The Lake in central Wisconsin, winter lasted from mid-November until May. As soon as the calendar acknowledged the vernal equinox elapsed in March or the actual temperature reached fifty degrees, every sunny day thirteen-year-old Cynthia would climb the attic stairs and crawl out onto the dormer deck with her beach towel and iodine mixed with peanut oil. She fastened sheets of tin foil with tape to the side of the house to reflect the sunlight. She began maintaining a bronze suntan year-round. Cynthia exhibited bronzed youth, possessed with sassy beauty.

*****

Harden, as far back as he could remember, lost his heart to The Lake. He loved the birthplace of his dear mother. Already known notoriously as Hardy, at age twelve bleak puberty now became his commencing query. Even after his mother died from cancer, he continued to visit his cousins at The Lake. Secretly, he languished for them. His full ripe first cousin, Cynthia, most frequently flowed into the lustrous foreground of his mind. His father began flying him and his younger brother, Mitchell, every summer to The Lake for a visit in June from their home in Connecticut.

With this summer's visit Hardy began to bring Cynthia real presents from the money he saved working for his father. They held hands walking toward the woods.

"You look so pretty today," he whispered to Cynthia.

"I sew most of my own clothes now in wool, silk, or soft cotton." She smiled at him. "I try to use a lot of shades of blue to show off my eyes. I made a special one of silk from scarves that Aunt Natty gave me. It has the colors of the sky in it. I'll wear it just for you, Hardy, to the barbecue cookout my mom is fixing for all of us tonight."

On their promenade returning to The Lodge, he planned to make notes about the clothes and colors she talked about in the secret black journal he kept. Hardy liked learning this information, keeping it in his black books since he learned to write.

They continued to hold hands. He pushed up his glasses with his free hand.

"Let's never stop playing our special Lady of The Lake game. When we're grown up, I'll buy you pretty real dresses in shades of blue to match your eyes and green to please my princess. I'm going to give you some real treasures today though. I found some pretty colored sparkling glass jewelry in the dime store at home. I told the lady in the store that I needed presents to take to my Aunt Natty in Wisconsin." He got them out of his swimming suit pocket where he hid them. "Here, here I have them. A sparkling green bracelet and a necklace with shiny blue glass stones on it," Hardy said. He held them forward, longing for her approval.

"Let me see. Oh, Hardy, they're so beautiful. I'll wear them secretly for now. Look at how they are glistening in the sunshine." She held the blue glass beads across her neck. "Thank you, thank you," she said, draping the bracelet across her left wrist.

He puffed up with a deep breath, relishing the fact that he pleased her.

"But you know what, Cynthia? I think that next year I'll ask Father if I can change my visit until August. Mitchell plays summer sports then until school starts and won't come. He doesn't care if he doesn't. The weather is better here then too."

"The weather would be better then for being outside," she agreed, squeezing his hand hard. "Hardy, climb out your window tonight after my dad says good night to me. I'll flick my light three times and have my screen unhooked for you to come through my window," Cynthia whispered to him. "I want to read you my school project I wrote about our ancestors. I got an A on it," she said proudly.

"Oh, Cynthia, will you read it to me really?" he asked in surprise.

"Yes, but we have to be sneaky, so no one knows we're up. If I don't read it to you tonight, we won't have another time. You're leaving tomorrow, early, I guess. Right?"

"Okay, I'll watch for your signal," Hardy said.

"Come on. We need to hurry now to get ready for Mom's barbeque," Cynthia said.

*****

Later that evening Cynthia sat on the pink purple-flowered bedspread on her bed, cross-legged. She gazed at the golden crescent moon rising above the Lake out her window. She held her school project on her lap to read again from this past year to trace her ancestral lineage.

"I'm giving you an A on your project, Cynthia," the teacher had said. "I know you worked hard on it. But I can tell you had special help composing it. The information you have gathered, Cynthia, you should keep to pass on to your children, one day when you are married."

It was true. A writer friend of Aunt Natty's wrote the manuscript after Cynthia organized it. Cynthia wanted the writing to be excellent. Put Put helped Cynthia by showing her letters written by his grandmother. Aunt Natty had saved her mother's diaries, along with old photographs, and shared them with her. Cynthia read the information in them over and over.

"Who's this?" Cynthia had asked Put Put when organizing her heritage project. She pointed at the faded sepia photo of a venturesome English merchant.

"That's your great-grandfather, Edward Parkton, when he came to The Lake in 1870," Put Put told her. "In those days after the Civil War, the news of the rich Wisconsin prairie land here surrounding The Lake was offered at $1.25 per acre. Almost free," Put Put said. "Yeah, it attracted the attention land-grabbers and homesteaders. However, 'Clever Ed' Parkton, as the reigning political machine called your great-grandfather after the war, didn't come like the other settlers. He infiltrated from the Carolinas, a moneyed man, bearing carpetbags filled with the fortunes of war," Put Put said with pride.

"And this, honey, is your great-grandmother, Agatha." Put Put held the worn photo at its best angle for Cynthia to see.

"She's very beautiful, isn't she, Daddy?" Cynthia said. "I look like her, don't I, Daddy?"

"Yes, yes, there is a real resemblance, except for her very blonde hair. Yours is just brown. You can still see how blonde her hair was in this photo," Put Put said.

"And, Daddy, it looks like she has jewels on."

"She was supposed to have jewels by the quart," Put Put said. "I think Natty ended up with some of them. I don't know."

"Aunt Natty never wears any jewels, Daddy," Cynthia said. "Maybe she's saving for me to wear when I grow up." Cynthia drifted off to sleep.

*****

Tonight sitting on her bed, Cynthia turned her bed light back on after Put Put said good night. She gave Hardy the all-clear signal.

"I didn't even hear you tiptoeing down the patio," she said, helping him in her window.

"You sit here on the floor, and I'll read." Cynthia returned to her perch on the bed. Hardy obeyed immediately, pleased to be chosen for such an event.

She began to read her manuscript.

Clever Ed, together with his wife, Agatha, purchased five hundred acres of gentle rolling slopes with rich black earth in 1870. He weeded out the options until he selected the most desirable land on the inlet water to The Lake. After choosing a site aloft the highest supreme crest, they spent eighteen months building a two-story frame house with fourteen rooms. It rose from a four-foot-thick white brick foundation. After sixty miles of transit, the brick arrived by wagon from the location of the firing kiln. Exquisite furnishings imported from European capitals adorned the interior. The magnificent home boasted the first indoor bathroom in Wisconsin, exhibiting imported white marble fixtures. Two colossal bronze lions that guarded the forefront entrance were stolen from the steps of a bank in the Carolinas. Above the entrance, designated in gold leaf, a magnificent inscription, "Golden Bounty," glistened in the sunlight. Crystal stemware shipped from European markets arrived intact etched with the likeness of the two guard lions. The finest wines flowed from France and Germany to fill the sparkling gold-rimmed goblets.

"Someday those gold-rimmed glasses with lions on them will be mine," Cynthia said to Hardy, keeping her voice soft. "I know Dad kept them. And, I'll drink champagne from them with my very rich husband. I'll have jewels by the quart." She hugged the manuscripts close to her chest in ecstasy thinking about it.

"I'll give you jewels too, Cynthia," Hardy said. "When I grow up, I'll be president of my dad's bank. I'll have lots of money to buy you presents."

"Oh, Hardy, I'll love all the presents you'll give me." She reached to him, touching his shoulder. He knew he would write notes in his journal about buying real jewels for her as soon as he secretly slinked back to his room.

She continued to read.

1926 Edward II, the first son born to Clever Ed, married. These future grandparents of Cynthia and Hardy acquired land and built a lake house on the east end of The Lake. The splendid shoreline afforded them cool prevailing winds and lazy summer sunsets over The Lake. Edward II and his wife, Gloria, became blessed with three children: Genevieve, the oldest and the future mother of Harden and Mitchell Alden; Edward III, the future father of Cynthia; and the youngest daughter, Natalie, the future parent of no one. Edward II with his wife skillfully incorporated upper loft space in the lake house to create living quarters for the summer frolicking of their three children.

"And now I live in this beautiful summer house—well, half restaurant," Cynthia said to Hardy, "with the pretty furniture from Golden Bounty. I'll read some more, Hardy," she said.

The 1930s and the Great Depression came together, bringing tenuous, thievish times. To avoid financial devastation, Edward II and Gloria opened the lake house to still-wealthy patrons to defray mounting expenses and property loss. Guests came to The Lake from the south by train with their children and nannies to escape the summer heat and disease. Rich travelers enjoyed weekends at the lake house from the not so far south, Chicago, and Milwaukee. Visitors signed the registrar from the northeast, Connecticut and New Hampshire. Edward II and his family remained resourceful in the Clever Ed Parkton fashion. Their lake house became known as The Lake Lodge, or just called The Lodge by the locals.

"We all still call it The Lodge," she said, smiling, smiling at Hardy. "Don't we?" she said. She had read the manuscript so many times it was almost memorized now.

She read on.

> *Golden Bounty laid prey for the Great Depression, becoming an offering to it, portions of it sacrificed for pennies. The county reclaimed some of its rolling fertile slopes for back taxes and auctioned them off. Some of the grandiose furnishings from Golden Bounty disappeared with vandals, stolen and sold. However, the Parktons managed to transplant a goodly portion of the luxurious furnishings to The Lodge. The added upstairs accommodations gained refinement and style. The keystone of the fieldstone fireplace in the great room read "Where friends meet hearts warm." One such friend vacationing from the northeast, George Alden, warmed Genevieve's heart, the oldest child of Edward II. He came from a self-made banking family. Knowing that the First National Alden Bank of Connecticut held its own through the Depression, Genevieve's parents lost sight of an appropriate time for a courtship. Genevieve quickly became the bride of George within the same summer of 1935. She left The Lake to begin her life as such in Connecticut.*

Spring 1949, Edward III, "Put Put"

Cynthia loved reading the part about her father.

> *In 1949 Edward III, the second child of Edward II, married a girl from Chicago whose family built a summerhouse after World War II at the Lake. In*

1951, Cynthia entered the world to them. Edward III basked in the old family heritage. He hunted, fished, swam, small-talked with eloquence, and swigged potions with the remaining Winnebago Indians. He delighted in life while conjuring up schemes for money. Some friends and family labeled him "Uncle Putter" or "Put Put Parkton" for all the avocations he could conjure up or put out. Others swore he acquired the pet name Put Put because as an infant he began fooling people by always putting his baby bottle out of sight. Growing up, Put Put learned to be resourceful and clever from his Parkton background.

Cynthia giggled.

"I can't imagine my father being a naughty, sneaky baby. Can you, Hardy?"

Hardy smiled broadly, shook his head no, and pushed up his glasses.

"Dad has told me about how his clever mother, Gloria, our grandmother, Hardy, ran the dining room at The Lodge," she said. "He said there would be a private dinner celebration scheduled in the dining room, and our grandmother would put a good-looking uncarved entrée in the center of the table sort of like a centerpiece. She would decorate it really pretty. The guests were so polite they wouldn't question carving or eating it. Then the next night the entrée would become the specialty of the house. So our grandparents would get paid twice for one thing. Get it?" She looked at Hardy.

"I think I do get it, Cynthia," Hardy said. "Two for one."

The two children smiled at each other with this information about how ingenious their grandparents were.

The last part in Cynthia's heritage manuscript, about her Aunt Natty, always thrilled Cynthia.

"Did you know Aunt Natty used her talent to marry a rich man?" Cynthia asked Hardy, leaning over on the bed to look directly at him. "You know by sewing all my own clothes so I always look rich, even if I don't have any money, will help me to marry a rich man. He'll think I'm rich."

"I'll buy you pretty clothes, Cynthia," Hardy stated, brave and arrogant. He crossed his arms across his chest, satisfied with his proclamation.

"Oh, Hardy, I know you will, forever. But I'll never be able to marry you. We're first cousins, and they don't allow it," she said.

"Yeah, I'm just a little kid, but I guess you can't marry a cousin or brother," he said. He rested his chin on his hands. His glasses slid down his nose a little, so he raised his head to look at his princess.

"Anyway, Hardy, there is just this last part about Aunt Natty I want to read to you, yet."

Natalie, "Natty"

Natalie, the third child of Edward II, Put Put's sister, and the future aunt of Cynthia and Hardy, acquired the pet name of Natty. With the name Natalie being a bit too formal for her, Natty fit her better because she could be as clever as the rest of the family, only more "nutty" in her mannerisms, and she could carry it off. She became an impressive swimmer in her own right. Natty spent her summers, beginning in early childhood, in the emerald waters of The Lake. As a teenager, she organized her own swim school, teaching aquatics off The Lodge dock.

"Elbows to the sky!" she sounded in the megaphone as apprehensive beginning swimmers attempted the Australian crawl.

Natty appeared reedy, yet penetrating, and convincing. Like her older brother, Put Put, she stood over six feet tall with strong, rangy arms. Although she graduated from Monapacataca High School in 1947, she did not leave The Lake until the fall of 1950 for a more adventurous course of life. A vital, sparky woman, she ventured off to Florida in pursuit of an aquatic career as a Wicky Wacky Girl in an aquarium. Underwater ballet, breathing through the long oxygen supply hose, gained her inordinate notability.

One day in 1952, while sitting at the upscale outdoor tiki bar adjoining the aquarium overlooking the sparkling white sand beach, Jeffrey Crestor, a gentleman rumored to be a rich Alaskan oil magnate, sat down beside Natty without an invitation. However, they had been introduced before at a social event at Club Bocana Beach. Her career afforded her opportunities to meet many flamboyant people of the wealthier class. Natty learned to love merrymaking posthaste. She imbibed with the best of them.

"Hello. I'm Jeff Crestor. I believe we've been introduced before. I must tell you I love watching you from outside the aquarium glass." He set his own drink on the bar. "How do your bangs stay so amazingly flat on your forehead? You're beautiful with the air bubbles framing your face. May I offer you another Kir?" Jeff asked her.

"Well, hello, Mr. Crestor. Yes, thank you, yes. I'd just love another Kir cocktail," she said.

"Another Kir for Miss Parkton and a Luksusowa with a splash, please. Shaken, not stirred." Jeff gave the order to the bartender.

"Yes, sir."

"Please, call me Jeff," he said to Natty. He focused his full attention on her.

"And Natty, please, to you. Aren't the swaying palm trees and the music enchanting together?" she said, leaning a little closer toward him. Being a tall woman, she knew this man stood taller than she did. She liked that, but not as much as the money rumors about him. The bartender placed the Luksusowa for Jeff on the bar and the fresh Kir cocktail in front of Natty.

"Thank you. Cheers, salud, and chin chin," she said. Raising the crystal goblet, she parted her sensuous pink painted lips to take a slow sip while giving Jeff direct eye contact. Her lips left a noticeable lipstick print on the sparkling gold-painted rim.

In the fall of 1954, Jeff finally proposed to her on a bent knee when she returned to Florida from The Lake. Summer always beckoned her heart to return to The Lake.

"Marry me, Natty," he said. "We will have our honeymoon ocean cruise around the world on the HMS *Queen Mary*. It's the ultimate cruise ship of the day, my love."

"I will, I will, I love you, I love you," she murmured. *And all your gushing oil wells in little ol' Alaska too*, she thought. She kissed him full on his mouth, leaving a blazing pink imprint. She withdrew his handkerchief, monogrammed JC, from his dinner jacket pocket and tenderly dabbed the lipstick away.

"What a contented man I am, my love, to know I found a woman who loves me, not just my money. I needed to be sure. That's why I waited two years to ask you to marry me. You're a patient woman, Natty."

*****

Cynthia closed her manuscript.

"That's all, Hardy. Isn't it wonderful?" Cynthia asked.

"Gee, yes, it really is, Cynthia," Hardy said. "I can see why you got an A on it."

She slid off her perch on the bed.

"Here, we'll move the chair over to help you get out the window."

He stood up, and she kissed him on the cheek. He beamed in her affection.

"Goodbye, Hardy, and we'll play Lady of the Lake when you come again the next time," Cynthia whispered to him.

"That will be wonderful, Cynthia, I'll bring you new presents," he said, bouncing on his heels.

"I know you will, Hardy," she said. She kissed him on the cheek again before his quiet climb out the window.

Cynthia turned off the light and pulled up her flowered comforter around her in bed. She gazed out at the crescent moon setting now.

Natty will be coming for the Fourth of July, she thought. *What fun it will be.*

CHAPTER 2

The Red MGA

Summer 1964, July Fourth Weekend

"Do you want to go for a ride?" Aunt Natty called to Cynthia while expertly maneuvering her glistening mahogany thirty-three-foot Baby Gar Wood to The Lake Lodge dock. She performed the landing simultaneously with a cigarette dangling from her dazzling pink lips, and she did not spill a drop of her Sunday morning Bloody Mary.

"Cynthia, the new neighbors, the Haleys, cordially invited me to have Sunday morning mint juleps at their Aunt Judith's summerhouse. I think they have them every Sunday morning all summer long. Come with me? It's only five miles down the north shore. What a gorgeous morning for a boat ride, darlink," she was still shouting above the gurgling noise of the Gar Wood engines.

Curvaceous Cynthia lay suntanning on The Lodge dock. Quick to accept the invitation, she raised herself up on the dock to one elbow at a ninety-degree angle.

"How nice of you, Aunt Natty," she happily called back. She looked at her reflection in the beautifully varnished mahogany boat. To be noticed in the Baby Gar Wood won hands down over a remote chance to be seen on the dock. "What should I wear?" Cynthia held her hands cupped around her mouth to direct the question to Natty.

"The way you are is fine, darlink. Just throw on a cover-up," Natty shouted back.

Cynthia, at the age of thirteen, already made heads turn and eyes focus. "Will you wait five minutes, Aunt Natty?" she called again, already on her way up to The Lodge to change her clothes for the ride.

"Yes, we'll wait, darlink." Natty shouted back. Her little dog, Sunbonnet Sue, yapped sitting next to her on the beautiful upholstered seat of forest green leather. Natty shut down the Baby Gar Wood, the name she chose to christen it, *Nutty Natty,* shown in gold leaf on the transom. In reality, the rumors of her husband's fortune in oil turned out to be founded in fact. This afforded her such luxuries as the Baby Gar Wood.

Natty sat comfortably in her boat stirring the Bloody Mary with her finger, hooking the ice cubes one at a time, flipping them in the water. After all, why dilute a good drink with melting ice?

*****

At Aunt Judith's summerhouse, the weekend before the Fourth of July 1964 started a week of picnics, parties, and an endless stream of guests. Mint had been gingerly plucked from its bed late yesterday afternoon on Saturday. Her young nephew Reginald Haley selected only the choicest sprigs just as the dew of the evening formed on it. He left the remainder for future Saturday evening plucking. Last evening Aunt Judith gradually stirred a pound of granulated sugar into ounces of hot water in a saucepan to make simple syrup. In silver julep mugs, she muddled the mint leaves together with the simple syrup. Then she filled the mugs with shaved ice and W. L. Weller Kentucky Straight Bourbon, Special Reserve, poured to the brim. Carefully she placed them in the freezer for an overnight stay, ready and waiting for Sunday morning.

Young Reginald's Aunt Judith built her summerhouse on The Lake before World War II on the exclusive north shore. The Sunday mint juleps carried on a precious family tradition. The past summers, her sister's family always visited Aunt Judith every weekend from Capital City with their young son Reginald. Reginald grew up on those weekends living and breathing every ripple on The Lake. This past spring Reginald's father, Al Haley, an attorney in Capital City, decided with his wife to sell their home and relocate to The Lake year-round. Attorney Haley opened his law practice in the nearby town of Belmont. Belmont also hosted a small, reputable private liberal arts college, Belmont College. Mr. and Mrs. Haley made arrangements for Reginald's admission for the fall term of 1964.

Natty, with Cynthia beside her, performed a precision landing at Aunt Judith's pier. She snugged her Baby Gar Wood behind the Haleys' twenty-two-foot 1948 Chris Craft Custom Sedan, christened *Temperance*. It sported a Chrysler Crown flat head, six-cylinder engine. Reginald admired Natty's skill in landing the big Gar Wood. He always yearned for a varnished mahogany Chris Craft. But their family boat, *Temperance,* was constructed of cedar and painted a predictable white and blue. Mahogany did not rejuvenate quickly after World War II from being used to make RAF Hurricane wooden fighter planes during the war. The *Nutty Natty,* constructed in the 1930s by Gar Wood, possessed two modern Chris Craft V-8 engines that replaced its original surplus World War I Liberty 500-horsepower aircraft engine. It could zip across The Lake like lightning. All the boat's original brass hardware glistened upon the varnished mahogany.

"What an adorable flowered sun suit you are donning, darlink," Natty said, and smiled at Cynthia after the landing. "You're already so tall and have the solid Parkton bone structure like Put Put and me."

"Thank you. I sewed it myself," Cynthia answered, pleasantly acknowledging the compliment, but she already knew she looked like a princess. Her hair, just a little blonde from the sun, framed her pretty tanned face. She exhibited a little peekaboo of her budding breasts.

"What kind of dog is that, again?" Cynthia asked, not familiar with little dogs.

"She's a Shih Tzu." Aunt Natty tenderly picked up her little dog from the after cockpit.

"I love that pink-flowered Lilly-designed ribbon tied to her collar." Cynthia patted the longhaired dog. "How can she see with her hair covering her eyes?"

"I don't know. I guess she can. The Egyptians supposedly used the Shih Tzus for guard dogs. I suppose she could be one for me, if I should ever need one." Natty laughed. "Come, darlink. Let's venture up to the party. My tongue is parched and waiting for a julep to soothe it. I'm sure they'll have lemonade, ice tea, or some such thing for you to drink too."

*****

Reginald Haley, at eighteen years of age, stood nearly six feet tall, looking good with a shock of sandy brown hair. His sharp, observant blue eyes sparkled behind contact lenses. He always complained that his legs were too short for his torso and often referred to them as "Haley legs." Reginald, now finally allowed mint juleps with the family on Sunday mornings, thoroughly enjoyed them. This suited him.

"Can I help you cleaning up again today, Auntie?" Reginald asked his Aunt Judith.

"Of course, my love. Thank you so much," she said.

There would be leftovers in every adult's silver julep mug. "Waste not want not," Reginald would proclaim to the empty service room. From the leftovers in frosted mugs, he would throw out the mint garnish and fancy straws, and then down the W. L. Weller.

Cynthia's arrival caused him to set down his silver julep mug. He watched her smile and laugh as she spoke comfortably to the adults while being introduced by Aunt Judith, together with Natty, on the outdoor terrace. Picking up his mug again, he quickly returned onto the terrace not to miss being introduced. His turn came, but he could not speak.

"What's the matter with you, Reginald? Cat's got your tongue?" Aunt Judith scolded. She shook her finger at him. "Shame on you for being so rude in front of this pretty young lady. We'll talk later. You and she are neighbors, you know. Your new house is only three houses down the lakefront from her family's, and their lodge." He lifted his mug, taking a huge chug. He could not believe his good fortune in learning this information.

The Parkton family, for the most part, now only utilized the upstairs accommodations during the summer. They opened the downstairs and great room for elegant evening dining under the care of a superb manager and chef, Mr. Silverfox. He resided in an upstairs apartment in the rear. Rumors ran rapid that The Lodge, currently in estate limbo with the passing of Natty and Put Put's parents, would soon be bailed out by Natty's new, rich husband.

Reginald said nothing that whole morning.

Fall 1964, Belmont College

As summer progressed, the trees reached their maximum foliage. Reginald's view of Cynthia on the third dock from his new home became totally obscured through his binoculars.

"Damn it! Something needs to be done about those trees, those damn overhanging branches, so I can see her," he fumed to himself. "I'll wait till Tuesday when there aren't many people around." The frustration of not having a crystal view of her became overpowering. "I'll give those low branches along the shoreline a good haircut." Before the foliage obstruction, when he could see Cynthia through his binoculars, he fondly began to call her budding breasts "B-Bs.".

Tuesday came, and he cranked up the chainsaw. After completing the tree's haircut, he boldly walked down to The Lodge dock where Cynthia lay sunbathing. "Well, that's more like it," he half mumbled as he flicked his cigarette ashes into the water.

Eyeing him, she sat up on one elbow. She adjusted her swimsuit top over her B-Bs. Cynthia, too, noticed Reginald. A private mutual admiration society formed between the two of them unbeknown to either one. She especially watched him driving his cute little red MGA.

"I like your fun red convertible. When do I get a ride in it, Reginald? My Aunt Natty likes it so much she said she found one similar to it in the auto classifieds for Capital City. It's black, and she calls it a MGA Twin Cam 1600, I think or something like that. She said she's going to buy it."

This information caught him off guard and drew his interest. "That would probably be a 1958, or so. An earlier model than mine."

"So when are you taking me for a ride in yours? I like yours." Sitting up on the pier now, she slowly moved the water with tanned feet and girly pink toenails. She smiled up at him.

"I'm going to t-take *Temperance* out..." Reginald stammered, continuing to walk down the pier to the slip where they moored it.

"Why did you cut the branches, Reginald?" she interrupted.

So I can see you better, beautiful, his mind said. "They told me to," his mouth said. He tried to keep his eyes focused on her in proper places, but he imagined his tongue flicking between her legs. He needed to get away fast. "Well, better get the boat," he exclaimed as he started his escape. Cynthia stood up, adjusted her swimsuit top again, and started prancing along right beside him on the dock. He could see himself in a striped jailhouse suit already.

"You could invite me, Reginald," she flirted.

"Your mother would never l-let you," he stammered, nervously flicking his cigarette into the water now.

"My dad would," she returned.

Put Put Parkton and Reginald had quickly befriended one another during the progression of the summer despite their age difference. Put Put's enjoyment and knowledge of the Lake with his quick and clever intelligence won Reginald's attention and admiration.

"You're probably right," Reginald agreed. Permission would be granted to the lovely Cynthia from her dad. Put Put would naturally think forbidding her a boat ride would be inexcusable.

"I'm picking up a couple friends, Connie and Billy," he responded, lighting another a cigarette.

"I know Billy. He's ahead of me in school. He's my friend, and I could be your friend too, Reginald," she flirted again.

"Another day we'll ask Put Put," he mumbled. *Damn it,* he thought to himself, *I am always mumbling and stuttering around her.* At least with the tree branches sawed down the frustration of not having a clear view of her brought relief. "I think I'll just scrap the boat idea and see if my friends Billy and Connie just want to meet me at Mid Point for a beer," he blurted out to Cynthia. Now his quickest escape became his house as he hurried away from her.

"Don't forget. Next time you'll ask my dad," she called after him, pulling up her bikini top to be sure it stayed in place.

*****

Mid Point proudly held an abstract back to the time Wisconsin became a state. Mid Point's class B tavern for eighteen-year-old beer consumption, and its grocery store stood side by side in the same structure. In front two gas pumps serviced the locals. In days gone by, rural residents bought provisions, a beer, something to eat, and could pick up their mail, all while having their animal feed ground. Now Mid Point enjoyed being the most frequented eighteen-year-old bar on the way around The Lake. The "lakies" and Belmont College kids all met and drank there.

Reginald first ran into Billy and Connie at the Paradise Park on the west end of The Lake in the beginning of the summer of '64. The kids their age all hung out at the park weekdays. Billy's grandfather's and Connie's parents' cottages were two miles apart by land route around The Lake. Both Billy and Connie enjoyed the privilege of no parents or family until the weekends.

"Hey, Billy, want to break out your fake ID and meet me up at Mid Point in an hour or so?" Reginald phoned Billy as soon as he returned to his house.

"Sure, but quit saying anything about my fake ID. Everybody thinks I'm eighteen. I'll see what Connie's up to." The threesome met later at Mid Point.

"I'm telling you, you should have seen her on the dock today. She asked me to take her for a car ride and to go out on the boat too. Do you believe it? And with those B-Bs of hers, thirteen," Reginald said and lighted a cigarette. "She's going to have the biggest tits in high school."

"Jail bait." Billy laughed smugly. He pushed his wavy chestnut brown hair back from his forehead. It grew long enough during the summer to curl up around his ears and his neck.

"Jeez, Reginald, aren't there enough girls around over eighteen? Especially you with that cute MGA," Connie chided, scrunching her freckled pug nose while guzzling her beer. "She's not even in high school, is she? I heard she's only going into eighth grade." Connie reached to the top of her head to be sure her long blonde hair hung straight down her back looped outside her leather visor. Being a slender young woman, she could wear the latest styles, but always stayed on the conservative, classy side. She wore traditional brown leather boat shoes today, not sandals.

"She's ready to be planked," Reginald retorted and smoked his cigarette.

"Well, I'll be gone and out of here when that happens." Connie changed the subject. "In less than a month now I'll be off to college in New York City." She started to sing, "Start spreading the news. I'm leaving today. New York, New York."

"Well, I'll be here all winter." Billy punched her lightly in the arm to shut her up. "I'm going to build a fireplace in my cottage."

"That's your grandfather's cottage," Connie broke in. "Why do you always say it's yours?"

"Or maybe I'll shoot down to the big shitty to help my mother with estate settlements," Billy rambled on, paying no attention to Connie's remark. "Mother does that sometimes for the lawyer she works for over in Belmont. I might help out in my grandpa's pharmacy in town for extra cash too. Just going to high school is way too boring. We'll do some drinking and have some parties at my cottage. Right, Reginald? All those college chicks you round up won't know I'm a year younger than you, especially with my own pad." Crossing his arms, he leaned back on his barstool grinning, pleased with himself.

"Jeez, Billy, you're so full of shit your eyes are brown," Connie said.

"Yep, that's their color all right, brown. No, actually, they're more hazel," he quickly teased her in response. "Like my new wire-rimmed sunglasses?" He kept the glasses on, wearing them inside. "Just trying to be cool like those Beatle guys. I told my grandfather to order a ton of them for this summer. They're going to big sellers. I think he's close to sold out already."

Connie shook her head at him. "I noticed you didn't take them off in here." Her own wire-rimmed sunglasses lay on the bar. "And it's not the big shitty. It's Port Michigan. You're so smart and don't do anything with it. You should get going your last year in high school and go to college the next year. Look at your grandfather, he's a pharmacist." Her clear green eyes crinkled up at the corners in irritation with him.

"I know, I know. I'm lucky to have him, and he lets me live at his cottage." Billy added, "Hey, it's another beer time."

*****

The colors of autumn began to flourish. In September, Reginald began his freshman year at Belmont College. He pledged the Sigma Alpha Epsilon Fraternity.

Five years younger than Reginald, Cynthia started eighth grade.

Autumn turned into winter. During the winter, Reginald and Billy compared the golden-haired girls on hair-dye box covers in Billy's grandfather's Rexall drugstore.

"What do you think of this color on Cynthia?" Reginald asked, holding up the box for Billy's opinion.

"With her knockers, it'd make her look like Marilyn Monroe." They both chuckled with pleasure about the possibility.

"Well, this will be the one then. She wants me to help her dye it for her fourteenth birthday," Reginald said.

Spring 1965, Cynthia and Reginald

Soon February and Cynthia's fourteenth birthday arrived. Cynthia's blonde summer highlights had totally faded from her mousy brown hair. She longed to be rich with beautiful blonde hair like her great grandmother, Agatha, before her. Out came the blonde hair dye secretly procured from Billy's grandfather's drugstore.

"Dad and my mother won't be home until late. It's a good time for you to come over to help me dye my hair, Reginald," Cynthia told him on the phone. He did not need to be asked twice.

After he arrived at her house, they made the preparations for the event.

"But don't you think we should read the instructions before we start?" she asked him.

"I only read instructions when all else fails," he answered. "Stick your head under the faucet and get it all wet. Then we dump the stuff in this first bottle on and wrap your hair up in this towel. You'll need to wait a few minutes. Then we pour on the second bottle for a little while, rinse the whole mess out, and zappady do da, you're a blonde."

"Okay, I'm ready with my towels," Cynthia said. She sat with the towel wrapped around her hair after the first bottle. "My head's getting hot," she complained.

"Then it's time to put on this bottle for a minute and we'll wash everything out." He poured. "Okay, it's on, and I'll wrap this towel on your hair for a minute."

"Reginald, my head feels like it's on fire."

"We better rinse it all out now," he said. He took off the towel to rinse. He stood back speechless at what he saw. He rinsed for a long time hoping it would be the answer.

"Reginald, it seems like you've been rinsing forever," she whined with her face down in the sink.

"Well, there's a bit of a problem that maybe rinsing will help," he stalled for a second, nervously rubbing his nose. Then he blurted out, "Your hair's blue."

"What do you mean my hair's blue?" She grabbed a hand mirror.

"IT'S NOT JUST BLUE, IT'S HYACINTH BLUE!" she screamed at him. "Get on the phone. Call Billy to bring another box of dye over here right away. Tell him another brand. Hurry!" she yelled at him.

"Holy cow, I've never seen you mad like this before. I'll call. I'll call." He raced from the bathroom.

"This time I'm reading the instructions and doing it myself!" she shouted after him.

He did not waste time calling Billy. Rather, he jumped in his car and raced to the drugstore himself. He returned posthaste with not one but three different brands. Cynthia grabbed one.

"What can anyone really do to me for dying my hair blonde?" She fumed, storming into the bathroom. "Expel me from school? Shave my head? Take away my birthday? Not allow me to see Reginald?"

So on her fourteenth birthday Cynthia became a silky and sunny blonde, and she knew she would always be one.

*****

Reginald's SAE Fraternity's spring party fell on the calendar in May.

"Cynthia, I really want you to go with me to my frat's spring party."

"Then you better ask my dad, not my mother."

Put Put, without concern, granted permission. "Fourteen is a good enough age as any for a girl to start dating," he said. Cynthia's mother waved the yellow caution flag unsuccessfully.

The town of Belmont, built on hills, stood in sharp contrast to the surrounding flat prairie land. The college existed on the west side of the town toward the Lake. The fraternity house, an old, original family home built of cream city brick, sat across the street from the town cemetery, which extended down a steep hill, called Thrill Hill by the college kids.

The May evening of the spring fraternity party arrived. Reginald appeared exactly at six, punctual as always, at Cynthia's door. He put the top down on the red MGA because of the unusually warm spring night for central Wisconsin. The fragrance of rose-colored crabapples filled the early evening air.

"Come, children, we need to take some pictures of you two in the living room. You look so pretty, dear, in that powder blue dress. What a beautiful job you did sewing it. The blue matches your eyes.

And your hair is lovely flipped up on the ends," her mother said, flitting around the living room and looking through her new Polaroid she bought special for the occasion.

Cynthia's blue-strapped dress had a matching shoulder jacket that shimmered with interwoven blooming pale purple and pink flowers in the fabric design. Like the dress she wore, Cynthia bloomed. Put Put did not mention a curfew as the young couple departed from the house for the evening.

"How do I look, Reginald?" Cynthia purred, comfortably sitting next to him. She smiled at him like Mona Lisa, but alluringly showed her snowy white teeth.

"Great...good," he stammered, trying to keep his eyes off her already tanned B-Bs peeking out above the powder blue field of silk. Even the jacket could not hide the tan outline on her B-Bs. She chimed and smiled again at Reginald in the topless red MGA. He kept the bottle of Mad Dog 20-20 hidden under his seat.

He parked across the street from the fraternity house against a convenient old tombstone in the cemetery to limit the risk of the car rolling down Thrill Hill. He left the transmission in first gear.

"Why did you park here of all places?" she asked. She did not want to walk far in her heels.

"The brakes. I gotta fix 'em one of these days," he said.

"Oh, is it safe?"

"Sure, sure," he answered.

Inside the frat house at the Spring Party, Cynthia held her own with poise and beauty despite her juniority to the college girls.

"I love your hair, and you're tanned so early in the season," an older girl complimented her in the bathroom. "I flew to Florida with two of my sorority sisters for spring break, but none of us are tanned like you are."

"Thank you," Cynthia said politely.

Reginald and Cynthia danced the slow numbers close together with his hand in the center of the small of her back, pressing her even closer to him. She did not resist. With only the barrier of clothes separating them, he could feel her body rubbing against his groin. After an hour of this sweet torture, they left the party. He kept her close to him with his arm tight around her waist as they walked across the street to the red MGA. The warm night moon-bathed under a sparkling clear sky. Cynthia slithered under the steering wheel into the unrestricted passenger seat. Reginald followed, not realizing he caught his trousers on the gearshift lever, shifting the car into neutral. The point of the planking imminently beckoned. Pressing forward, he asserted the plunderage, an operation of teamwork. Reginald, a true depredationist, filled with love for her at the same time. The red MGA rock 'n' rolled against the tombstone, finally knocking it down. At this point of the planking, Reginald regained his senses. He realized a slow descent down the Thrill Hill beginning. Cynthia, too, recovered her senses. Her skirt now glimmered in the moonbeams with red fire-like wet confusion to it. Her maidenhood finished forever.

After that evening, the red MGA spent summer evenings during the summer of '65 at the outdoor movie theater between Belmont and The Lake. It did the "Reginald and Cynthia rock 'n' roll."

Cynthia started her freshman year at high school that fall. Reginald started his sophomore year at Belmont College.

Spring 1966, Vietnam Looming

In the spring of 1966, Reginald escorted Cynthia to her first high school prom. At age fifteen, she looked luscious and candy coated with her freshman year in high school nearly completed.

They left the prom early.

"It'll always be you, Cynthia," he said, holding her close in the parked car by The Lake. "You're the love of my life."

He remained the deflowering ravisher, but smitten with his love for Cynthia. She penetrated his mind, continually making him overflow with true affection for her. "We'll be going to the outdoor movie again as soon as it opens. Probably Memorial Day weekend."

"That'll be good," Cynthia said. "My mother likes it so much better when we're actually doing something like going to a movie. It's a date then you know."

*****

In the summer of 1966, Connie came back from New York to continue college the coming fall in Port Michigan and work in her parents' rental business. Reginald and Billy discussed ways to avoid the Vietnam draft with Connie over a couple of beers at Mid Point. The three all talked about it, acutely aware of the Vietnam draft looming.

"I'm going to figure out a way to avoid the draft without going to Canada," Billy grumbled. "Maybe I'll become a card-carrying minister. Yeah, maybe that would work."

"You a minister...ha." Connie shot him a sideways look that spoke the words a second time.

In September when Reginald started his junior year at Belmont College, his unfortunate anticipation proved correct. "Greetings from the President of the United States of America" arrived. "Oh, shit," he said, taking it nonchalantly in stride.

In 1967, immediately after his junior year, he left for boot camp at Fort Campbell, Kentucky, in the United States Army. Cynthia wrote to him twice. Then she shifted into meeting summer people and particularly the young, good-looking guys that came from rich families. Reginald spent four months at Fort Campbell. From there he went to Fort Leonard Wood for Advanced Infantry Training. In the fall, with lots of time now, Cynthia began to write back to him every time she received a letter from him. The summer people had all pulled out Labor Day weekend. In November Reginald wrote that at the end of January his furlough home started for six weeks before being shipped to "The Nam." Elated, she read one part of his letter over and over again. It said, "I'll have lots of money to take you out and even buy you some presents. There's nothing here to spend my pay on except cigarettes, and they're real cheap. My hair is all cut off, though. I'll look real different."

She wrote back, "I just can't wait to see you. You'll be here for my birthday. Maybe a surprise present? How exciting. Oh, Reginald, we'll have so much fun again and go out all the time. I don't care about your hair all cut off."

*****

Reginald's furlough came and went. The sun painfully rose on the frightful morning of Reginald's flight. Billy drove the red MGA down to Port Michigan for the plane to Travis Air Force base for further transport to Vietnam. Reginald and Cynthia huddled and held each other in the passenger seat.

"I'm nothing but fresh cannon fodder," Reginald uttered, still drunk from the night before. Cynthia and Billy didn't stay to watch his plane leave. They drove away because they could not stand it.

Later that day Connie, at home in Port Michigan, answered her ringing telephone.

"I'll never forget today," Billy spoke pensively, unusual for him, then paused. "What a damn numbing morning to the nth degree. Cynthia cried miserably all the way down. Funny, I never thought she could be broken up. Reginald grumbled away, still drunk. He kept going on and on about no remains. The most shitty, horrible, saddest, saddest day."

"Let's hang up. It's too hard for me to talk right now," Connie managed to choke out. Her head turned side to side with tears welling in her eyes.

CHAPTER 3

Kissing Cousins

Summer 1969, Aunt Natty and Reginald's Return

Dear Aunt Natty, together with her wealthy husband, bought The Lodge out of the Parkton estate. Immediately they hired Mr. Silverfox for both positions of chef de cuisine and general manager. In the transaction, Natty managed to keep the substantial side lot next to The Lodge in her name only, in the resourceful Parkton fashion. In addition, she procured life tenancy in her name only of The Lodge's largest suite with a lake view on the south side of the building toward her lot. The life tenancy granted her the unusual right to pass it on to an heir. A formal living area welcomed guests upon entering from the interior ascending staircase adjacent to the fireplace from the cocktail lounge of The Lodge. Just inside the entrance, a hallway to the left led to three bedrooms and two baths. A vintage porcelain bidet gleamed white in the master bath. An immediate pocket door to the right of the entrance opened to the Pullman kitchen. The dining area at the other end of the kitchen overlooked the Lake. Natty immediately added a screened porch across the dining room toward The Lake. A second exterior entry with outside stairs rose from the brick walkway below to the French double-door entrance into the porch. The roof of the porch, constructed with thirty-inch overhangs in the old manner, did not require gutters. She ordered cantilevers constructed for a bright, airy sunroom off the dining room to the south. Natty purchased old trolley car windows while on a shopping spree in San Francisco. She shipped them to The Lodge COD, much to the chagrin of Mr. Silverfox. The vintage poured-glass windows arrived totally intact. When their installation was completed, the polished glass intermingled its pastel hues of purples, blues, greens, and pale yellows in the sunlight. Looking through them to view Natty's gardens in her south side lot, made the flowers appear as a Renoir painting. She liked this. Her sunroom drew profuse attention from her guests.

"It demonstrates your refined taste," they complimented her graciously.

Below the dining room, she ordered the construction of two distinct garden areas visible from her porch. Natty spent every morning in them to plant and nourish a vegetable and another flower garden. She loved to dillydally with a cocktail or a bottle of vintage wine in the gardens, or anywhere for that matter. Also, she retained with her life tenancy two boat slips on the pier in the still waters behind Deer Island owned by The Lodge.

Natty and her husband resided the majority of the year at their main home in Alaska. However, Natty frequented her suite at The Lodge solo during the summer season. She passed the requirements for a private pilot's license and now flew a Cessna Citation, her own plane named *Powder Puff*. She also competed in the Ladies Powder Cup flying races in Florida. Natty and her husband maintained two residences in Florida with northern and southern locations respectfully. The one in South Beach he titled only in her name.

When visiting The Lake, she would land the plane at nearby Oshburg.

Mr. Silverfox became a nervous wreck whenever she asked him to fetch her upon her arrival. Her scandalous behavior caused him great consternation as it conflicted with the refined image he created at The Lodge.

"I'm so relieved Reginald Haley returned to us unscathed from Vietnam in the middle of June, and I insist that you hire him for the bar management position at The Lodge as soon as I tell him to inquire about it," Natty informed Mr. Silverfox. "I'm staying for all of August to orchestrate the business dealings, darlink. You'll need my advice about managing."

Mr. Silverfox began to break out in hives.

"I'll take care of it. I'll hire him. But I'll be sure he understands the rules. There's no drinking while on duty, a strict dress code, and no second chances," Mr. Silverfox grumbled back at her. A rash started to creep into his armpits.

"Well, despite the age difference, I've felt quite at home with him ever since I met him when his family moved to The Lake. Being my new neighbor then, he helped me out immensely with small chores. He's so responsible. He always seemed to have time for me. And we just loved consuming copious quantities of toddies on the dock together." She stuck a cigarette between her parted feisty pink lips and handed her gold Dunhill lighter to Mr. Silverfox. He felt the rash creeping down his right arm, but lighted her cigarette. Exhaling the first drag of smoke toward him, she said elated, "Won't we be lucky to have him working under the same roof where we all live, darlink?"

August 1969, Harden Alden

Reginald began his new job at The Lodge and tended bar for the cousins Cynthia and Hardy when they met there that first night of Hardy's annual August visit. His eager eyes followed Cynthia as she mingled with locals at the bar. Watching her, Reginald could only hope she would steal extra time to talk to him, alone.

For this summer visit to The Lake, Harden and his wife, Nan, arranged to dine with Cynthia and her new husband, Larry Young, at The Lodge the first night. When they met, Hardy planted his hand assertively in the center of Cynthia's back, locking his first cousin in an elongated kiss on the mouth. Cynthia showed off her golden tan, wearing a stark white miniskirt with a matching top. One fluorescent pink stripe ran up the center of the ensemble with emphasis around the plunging deep-V neckline. They kissed in front of the fieldstone fireplace with the keystone that read "Where friends meet hearts warm." This great room, now The Lodge's elegant cocktail lounge, overlooked The Lake to the west. A lady pianist in a formal royal blue floor-length dress played classical music selections at the grand piano.

Hardy, slight in build, stood five feet ten inches tall now. Against the white of his other fingers and hands, his right index and middle fingers showed a noticeable yellow stain from cigarette smoking. Except for the cigarette stains, for a man, his hands and fingers looked delicate. His teeth, too, fine and precise, displayed a jaundice-like color. The black horn-rimmed glasses he wore looked garishly unbecoming, especially against his pink complexion and white-blond hair. The eyebrows, however, were ragged and undefined from unconsciously pulling out the hairs one at a time behind his horn-rimmed glasses. Stress and fantasies did that to him. From time to time, his cigarette got in the way, singeing hairs, bringing him back to reality.

Cynthia pulled away from Hardy, but not before he whispered, "Tomorrow, lunch at Noble's."

Cynthia nodded slightly. Then she reached for Larry's hand. "Hardy, this is my husband, Larry Young." She had become a creamy brimming, early June bride after high school graduation. "Larry, this is my cousin, Harden Alden, and his wife, Nan."

"And this is our precious baby, Amber. We did appreciate your beautiful wedding pictures," Nan nervously interceded. "I'm sorry we missed your wedding. You know Hardy likes to make his annual visit to The Lake in mid-August. We'd already made all the plans when the invitation arrived. Both June and August could not be fitted in this year." Missing Cynthia's June wedding agreed with Nan, as she never delighted in observing Hardy when he socialized with his cousin. The excuse worked for Hardy, too, with no desire whatsoever to witness his cousin's wedding.

Despite Cynthia, Nan liked returning to The Lake every summer to visit with her family at their lake home. Her family started vacationing there several decades ago. Hardy met Nan on one of his visits to The Lake. He continued to court her, marrying her two years later. This special 1969 summer's visit, she possessed the product of her union with Harden: little baby Amber. Nan's family, ever so anxious to see the new arrival, welcomed the forthcoming visit. Cynthia dismissed the baby with a polite but uninterested smile. She excused herself to move on through the room to mingle. Nan proudly carried little Amber to the dinner table reserved for them, leaving Harden to chat with Larry.

*****

"Will you please try to be back for lunch with the family?" Nan implored to Hardy the next day.

"Let's play it by ear," Hardy told his wife. "You know I want to get out to run some errands while I'm here. This morning seems like a good time." He left the house to meet Cynthia at Noble's at noon. It remained the restaurant and bar of choice that the lake people frequented the most. Perfectly located on the north side of the water, Noble's established itself close to the Lake's quaint, beautiful downtown. Its location also supplied ample boat docking facilities, making it a favorite of the lake people and yachting events. The entire dining room provided tableside seating with a view of The Lake to the east. The restaurant offered an excellent menu, prepared by the French chef Luis. The menu seldom changed though the years.

Upon meeting, Harden and Cynthia embraced briefly then sat at the bar area. She liked to sit near the entrance so she could be seen. She wore a flowered tie-dyed sundress, mid-calf in length, with matching wedge-heeled shoes. She tossed the matching jacket onto the barstool next to her. The sundress strap tied behind her slender neck revealed her bare golden back. This sexy summer ensemble required no bra. Her tan and blonde hair combination could not have complemented the ensemble more if it had been painted in a picture. The bartender, their friend Billy Benwolfski, spotted the couple right off. He immediately came over.

"Hi, Billy, how's it going?" Cynthia beamed radiantly at her former upperclassman schoolmate.

"It's going the best...the best. And how is the blushing bride? Still blushing or just a bride?" he joked. "Jeez, you sure look good. But then, you always do. Marriage must agree with you. I guess I haven't seen you in a year. A year sure goes by fast," Billy said.

"Time does fly, doesn't it," she said and smiled sweetly at Billy. "An ice tea, please, Billy. No sugar. Just a wedge of lemon."

"And, Hardy, it's good to see you again too. It must be annual visit time. Of course, I heard you were coming. The naked lake's grapevine let the word out. It's usually right. Still Jim Beam and water, Hardy?" Billy questioned him.

Hardy nodded yes to the Jim Beam and water, lighting a cigarette.

"Good to be back," Hardy said.

"Okay, drinks right away," Billy said, setting out the correct beverage glasses.

"Hardy, your daughter is adorable," Cynthia complimented Hardy, turning toward him. "She has your blue eyes and blonde hair. Nan dressed her up in such a cute little outfit."

"She is good," he answered, gazing at Cynthia. She now rested her head on the top of one tanned hand, returning the eye contact with a come-hither look. He reached into his summer sport coat pocket and pulled out a small wrapped package.

"Oh, thank you, Hardy," she purred, opening the package. "How do you remember Channel Number Five is my favorite...you never forget anybody's birthday either."

He still kept his secret journals and made notes about people, always the voyeur.

"When did Reginald get back from Vietnam?" he asked, pushing up his glasses. "Surprised me to see him tending bar at The Lodge last night," he remarked.

"Um...in the middle of June," she replied thoughtfully.

Harden downed his first JB and water. He rubbed out his cigarette and lighted another.

"Another there, Hardy?" Billy asked.

"Sure. Hey, look at that." Hardy chuckled, smiled, and gestured toward the lake. "Cynthia…wow, that's Connie. Long time no see… can you dig that boat?"

Reginald and Connie docked at the pier in Reginald's Aunt Judith's 1966 twenty-foot Chris Craft Sea Skiff, white with a blue cove stripe, which set off the blue leather interior.

They tied up and entered Noble's from the dock door. Spotting Cynthia and Hardy, they slid their way through the crowded bar over to them at the parking lot entrance.

"Good to see you last night. What do you call that doorstop you produced?" Reginald asked and shook Hardy's hand.

"Amber. The doorstop is a girl," Hardy stated proudly, smiling, showing his tobacco-stained teeth. "Let me buy you all one."

"She's such a beautiful blonde baby with Hardy's blue eyes," Cynthia contributed, acknowledging the two new arrivals.

"Congratulations, Hardy," Connie exclaimed. "Great to see you again, really good." They exchanged a warm, friendly hug.

"It's been a while. What, it's been about two summers since we've seen each other. Right?" Hardy questioned Connie. "Missed you the summer you were in New York."

"Yeah, yeah, too long, Hardy," she thoughtfully responded. She changed the subject. "What are you and Cynthia up to today? Cynthia, you look great, what a neat outfit."

"Thank you. We wanted a little time to talk to each other without all of our families with us," Cynthia said. "Cousins need to do that. Lots of changes for both of us in the last year. Big changes… marriages and babies." She smiled warmly at Hardy while gently placing her hand briefly on his shoulder.

"Hey, where did you steal that boat from, Reginald?" Billy kidded him from the other side of the bar. "Going to tell us it's your boat, just like I tell all the chicks my grandpa's cottage is mine?"

"Watch my nose grow," Reginald retorted with a guffaw. "Just call me Pinocchio."

Everyone laughed, knowing Billy handed out the bull, not Reginald.

"How about our drinks? Hardy says he's buying," Reginald quipped.

"What a gathering of the clan. What are you guys going to have? Reginald, rum and coke?" Billy asked.

"Meyers Rum, if Hardy's buying," Reginald interjected.

"Connie?"

"Maybe just a beer."

"And another Beam and water there, Hardy? You're okay, Cynthia? Boy, it's really busy today," Billy said. "The bar crowd today reminds me of one of my favorite stories your dad told about himself and his Indian pal Slow Knocker, Cynthia." She delivered an interested look to him. Billy took the encouragement and continued. "They were supposed to be blood brothers, you know. Put Put sure knows how to chuck and jive, doesn't he?"

Cynthia giggled and rested her elbow on the bar with her chin on the back of her tanned hand. Hardy shuffled his feet and pushed his glasses up looking at her.

"One time, he told me when we were hunting together about a particular hot summer day when he and Slow Knocker were drinking whiskey and fishing out of the canoe." Billy paused to see if he had his four friends' attention. "Hey, let's play fool the tourist tonight, Put Put told me he said to Slow Knocker," Billy told them, gaining enthusiasm in his delivery. "That was one of Put Put's favorite shrewd games to pull off for extra cash, you know," Billy continued speaking. They all did know, knew the story, but loved it and would gladly listen again.

"Put Put told me that Slow Knocker said, 'Yeah. That's good. I will. I can use a few extra dollars. I'll wait for you,'" Billy rattled on. "Late that afternoon in Noble's, Put Put proclaimed in a loud voice to the customers that he could swim underwater all the way across the bay to The Lodge." Billy imitated Put Put's proclamation from behind the bar, immediately gaining the attention of more patrons at the bar.

"Yeah, sure you can," a fat man with a martini in his hand yelled back at Billy.

"Not me, another guy, Put Put, the dude in the story," Billy shouted to the fat guy, laughing.

"It was a very crowded afternoon, like this," Billy said, raising his voice as he gained other listeners.

"Luke, the bartender that afternoon, said to Put Put, 'You're going to swim it again tonight?' The bartender chuckled. 'That's a strong two miles across the bay.' Luke purposely said it real loud to spark the curiosity of the tourists. He knew he would get payback from Put Put," Billy said, continuing with the story.

"You? You'll never make two miles," a painted lady on a barstool next to the fat man hooted at Billy.

"The bar crowd joined in the banter with Luke," Billy said, ignoring her and raising his voice for everybody in the area to hear. He poured forth his story with gusto.

"'You guys should bet against him. I'll get something to write on and take your names and bets. If he doesn't make it, I'll pay double,' Luke said above the bar noise and egged the patrons on more," Billy exclaimed to his attentive listeners at the bar.

"'Sure, sure. Who wants to bet against me? Come on. Place your wagers against me,' Put Put proclaimed and baited them more," Billy whooped.

"'I'll go get my swimming suit on and be back by dinnertime,' Put Put shouted at the eager people wagering bets with Luke." Billy liked a fired-up crowd. It meant tips for him.

"Early in the evening as the sun set, Put Put dove into the Lake from Noble's pier with the tourists watching intently." Billy now had at least ten bar customers listening, along with his friends. "Put Put immediately disappeared from sight in the green waters." Billy waved his hand in the air toward the lake.

"Hey, tarbender. How about another cocktail here," a sunburned tourist brand-new to the area waved his empty glass at Billy.

"More drinks? Sure." He hustled to satisfy the customers. *I should get some good tips out of this*, he thought.

"The long swim finally commenced." Billy's voice became louder and excited as more people were listening. He became dramatic and humorous in his rendition.

"Billy is a one-man show," Cynthia said to Connie. "He's as good as the story." They both laughed. Hardy pushed up his glasses totally amused. This was his favorite story about his uncle Put Put.

"The spectators from here hurried to drive to The Lodge and await Put Put's arrival at the dock. Put Put's Indian blood brother, Slow Knocker, hidden by the pier's shadow, waited without a sound in his canoe. Put Put easily glided underwater to the waiting canoe. His friend then paddled him briskly across the bay to the other side while he clung to the canoe's railing. Moonbeams started to dance like liquid diamonds on the darkening water." *This is great. Money for me.* Billy punched the jukebox knob to turn it down. "Slow Knocker saw the nearness of The Lodge dock. He tapped twice with his paddle to signal Put Put." Billy knocked hard on the bar. "Put Put tapped back." Billy thumped the bar again with his bar rag. "Then Slow Knocker expertly maneuvered his canoe in the darkness under the camouflaging limbs of a willow tree." Billy lowered his voice. "Slow Knocker knew his way through the rushes in the water from the previous times. Put Put easily swam the breaststroke underwater the remaining distance to the anxious waiting tourists on The Lodge dock."

"'I did it,' Put Put yelled, popping up out of the water." Billy jumped up suddenly. Connie and Cynthia began laughing. "He smugly collected the wagers in the bar of The Lodge," Billy clattered on. "The duped tourists, with parched throats from the long wait on the dock, flooded the bartender with orders. Inevitably, they spent the remainder of the evening at The Lodge bar, not to return to Noble's. End of story." Billy proclaimed.

"Bravo," an older man wheezed, throwing some money on the bar.

"I loved it, and right here at Noble's." A young woman batted her fake eyelashes at Billy and slipped him some paper money. More money and coins clanged on the bar from the raucous crowd.

"Hey, Billy, I've always said you're good at the bull, but we only have time for one here, because Reginald needs to get to The Lodge for work," Connie insisted. "But maybe we'll take tagalongs for the boat ride over."

"And I'm not swimming underwater either," Reginald said, hoping to get at least a look from Cynthia.

After finishing the round at the bar with Hardy and Cynthia, Connie and Reginald ordered their carryouts for the boat. The two left in the Chris Craft. Hardy and Cynthia continued their conversation at the bar.

"So what do you think about tomorrow night? The four of us having dinner at The Lodge once more?" Hardy questioned. "It will be all right with Nan."

"I'd like that so much, Hardy," she murmured. "I have something stunning to wear that no one has seen." For a moment their eyes sensuously locked. "I'm sure it will be all right with Larry. But let's ask Aunt Natty too. You know she would love to be included by her favorite niece and nephew."

*****

The following evening from behind The Lodge bar, Reginald again observed Hardy planting his hand in the center of Cynthia's back, exchanging an elongated mouth-to-mouth hello kiss. Strangely Reginald watched betrayed, yet taken aback by her beauty. She wore a cream-colored flowing bell-bottom pantsuit, with large hand-embroidered azure forget-me-nots around the bottoms of the bells. The paler shade of the blue silk halter top emphasized her tan, making the total package extremely pleasing to the eye. Reginald cordially attended to Harden, Nan, Cynthia, and Larry's drink orders before their dinner.

"See a lot of action in Vietnam, Reginald?" Larry asked.

"Nope, when they figured out that I could type, I instantly became the company clerk at Fort Leonard Wood. Then in Vietnam, I became a battalion clerk again. Twenty-Fifth Admin Company, Headquarters, Twenty-Fifth Infantry Division. Just kept records of the company. My action consisted of a desk and a typewriter. That's all."

"You mean you never saw any fighting over there?" Hardy looked at him, astonished.

"First six months I lived in a hooch. It's a Quonset hut, fifty feet long with a half-moon roof made of galvanized steel welded together. About twenty-five guys and beds in the hooch. Yeah, we all had a hooch maid. My hooch maid was pregnant from the guy before me, so no sex. She didn't want the baby to have two fathers. Didn't understand that, but that's it."

Hardy and Larry snickered. They were a little uncomfortable with their wives at their sides, but wanted to hear more. Harden's wife blushed, tilting her head away.

"Excuse us, but I think that Nan and I will go to the piano bar and request a show tune. Join us when you're finished with your seedy talk about babies having two fathers." Cynthia shot Reginald a contemptuous look. All three men's eyes followed Cynthia momentarily. Reginald caught himself and continued talking after the ladies left.

"There were sandbagged bomb shelters next to the hooch. Nope, first six months, there were a few rockets occasionally. Never saw a bullet from the time I got off the airplane at Cam Ron Bay. Never saw round-eyed women either. That's about it," Reginald concluded.

"Good God man, what did you do over there all that time?" Hardy smoked his cigarette amazed.

"The R and R was great. You turned your MPC—you know, Military Pay Currency—for green backs. For fifty dollars you could get a girl in Bangkok. If you did not like the one you got the first night, you exchanged her and got another. The first one gave me the clap. I started pissing fire."

Hardy pushed his glass forward, indicating he wanted a refill. The men glanced at their wives at the piano bar; they seemed to be content singing show tunes now along with the lady pianist. The men were primed to hear more.

Reginald rubbed his hand nervously over his nose. "Yeah, the second girl was great. You could keep them for twenty-four hours or a week. But I could never get used to the chicken gizzards they liked to chew all the time, like chewing gum." Reginald turned his head to the side, chewing and making a noisy chomp-chomp sound. "No English. Somehow you figured it out. Easily you could understand each other in the dark," he added with authority. "But when these girls were done, they were really done, finished. Cast out of their society. Let me tell you about Vung Tau. It's an old French resort area on the South China Sea at the mouth of the Mekong River. Just like a postcard. I hired a driver, Mr. Hue, who would take me anywhere I wanted. You could walk along the beach, except there were shell casings smashed all over the seashore." He faltered, his mouth dropped open, looking past them. "Oh boy, look at that. She's blasted."

Larry and Hardy turned to see the unexpected spectacle. Aunt Natty swaggered down the flight of stairs from her apartment to the cocktail lounge balancing an empty martini glass on her head. She wore a shocking pink and lime green Lilly Pulitzer cocktail dress. The pink in the dress matched her blazing pink lips. Under her arm she clutched her little Shih Tzu dog, Sunbonnet Sue, with a bold pink and white Lilly scarf tied to her collar.

Aunt Natty plopped Sunbonnet Sue on the bar and took the martini glass off her head.

"Fill'er up." She grinned at Reginald, leaning over the bar for him to light her cigarette. "Hardy, come give your Auntie Natty a big kiss, darlink. Here, Larry, light my cigarette. Never mind. It's already on fire. But make yourself useful for once somehow, and stop staring. Yippee, so I've had a couple. Have one, Larry, it could only improve you. Oh, never mind. You probably can't be improved." Larry stood ridged, speechless. "Now, Hardy, where is Auntie's kiss?"

Hardy pushed up his glasses. Hugging her, he kissed her on the cheek, avoiding those fluorescent lips.

"That's better, darlink, better. Have a cocktail."

"Aunt Natty, it's so nice to see you. You look marvelous in that Lilly."

"Thank you, darlink, thank you. Hardy, you always love all my Lillys. Where is your cocktail, Reginald?"

"You know Mr. Silverfox's rule about not drinking while on the job."

"Well, I'm the owner here and he's the manager. I'm changing the rule and buying you one. I said have a cocktail." Reginald quickly dumped together a Meyers and Tab. "Now, bumps." She held up her filled martini glass. Hardy, Larry, and Reginald held up their cock-tails to toast with her.

"Bumps," they all said in unison.

"We should see how the girls are doing," Hardy said. He shot a look at Larry. Then he nodded at the cringing Mr. Silverfox, indicating to seat them soon.

"Yeah, good idea. Catch you later, Reginald," Larry agreed, throwing some money on the bar for Reginald.

"Larry, do something. Carry Sunbonnet," Natty demanded. She passed him the little Shih Tzu.

"Can I take your drink for you to the table, Aunt Natty?" Hardy began to reach.

"No, no, darlink. I am always the master of my own libation, so it doesn't get away from me." She laughed. Hardy took her elbow and compelled her toward the dining room and away from the piano bar.

"Shouldn't we sing a few show tunes first, darlink?" Natty asked him. "I'm getting married in the morning. Ding dong, the bells are going to chime," Natty started to sing her favorite show tune. She hesitated and looked toward the piano bar. "I'd like to sing some songs, Hardy. Now don't argue with me, darlink."

"Maybe later, Natty, because Larry is collecting the girls to join us right now at the table," Hardy said gently yet definitely guiding her toward the dining room.

Mr. Silverfox bit his lips as he watched that unshackled woman stagger into his dining room. She acted like she still lived in The Lodge and not just the suite.

"Let's see. That mirror over on the far wall. I forgot that and need it in my suite. What? No chair for Sunbonnet Sue?" Natty glared at Silverfox.

"Please, get a chair," Hardy said to Mr. Silverfox. Hardy tried to remain calm, pushing up his glasses twice. Mr. Silverfox pursed his lips in a tight line. He left, but a minute later, he returned with a chair.

The hostess guided Cynthia, Nan, and Larry carrying Sunbonnet Sue to the table. As they passed the bar, Reginald's eyes, satiated with love, followed Cynthia.

"Cynthia, darlink, you are just fabulous in that electric blue bell-bottom outfit. It's quite fetching. You could certainly upstage Cher. The fabric could use some twinkle pink pattern intertwined, though, for oomph. I'll look through my Lilly fabrics and see what I can find for you. Don't you think so, Hardy? And, Nan dear, how is your lovely family?"

"They're very well, thank you, Natty. They're so pleased with Amber. Aren't they, Harden?" Nan emphasized his name at the end of her reply to break his daydream gaze at Cynthia.

*****

On the Saturday before his departure back to Connecticut, Hardy met Cynthia at Mid Point for a cocktail one last time. She wore a crimson red miniskirt ensemble with a short-sleeve red silk blouse and a matching red visor. Pushing up his glasses, he took a long look at her, casually observing that she had no panty lines.

"How is everything really going with Larry?" Hardy asked Cynthia, lighting a cigarette, anxious to hear the answer.

"I never should've married Larry. He's a drip like Aunt Natty says. But I thought with his family being so rich it'd be nice," she confessed to Harden. "And now, I am pregnant." She sighed, becoming teary-eyed. She looked at Hardy like a greenhorn babe. Hardy ordered a Jim Beam and water and took a long drag on his cigarette.

The confessional continued. She blurted out to him about her night in the cemetery in the red MGA. "Oh, how I wish it could be Reginald's." Hardy imagined his sweet-tempered cousin sitting next to himself in the red MG, dressed in her red miniskirt with no underpants and matching red visor. He lighted another cigarette with one already burning in the ashtray.

He knew Aunt Natty purchased that black MGA 1600 Twin Cam that was similar, or even better, than the red MGA. The magnitude of his reaction to Cynthia's confession exploded the depth of his imagination. Yes, he would talk to his Aunt Natty about her MGA 1600 Twin Cam after leaving Mid Point.

He drove straight to Aunt Natty's apartment on his way back to Nan's parents' cottage.

"You're in Alaska most of the time now. How about selling your MGA to me?" he asked Aunt Natty. "I could talk to Billy Benwolfski about storing it in his grandfather's barn. You store *Nutty Natty* there, too, don't you? I'd have a car whenever I come out here then. It would be great, great."

"I really have no use for that car now anyway, darlink. I'll just sign it over to you. You don't have to buy it. I agree it would be a plus for you to have a car here whenever you come." She handed him the keys on the spot.

*****

The following morning, Hardy found himself driving the eight-mile distance to Belmont in his black MGA. Over the slightly rolling countryside he raced. His mind swilled in the flight of fancy. He found the SAE fraternity house. The cemetery extended down Thrill Hill. He fixed his gaze on the tombstone that still lay on the ground. Little by little, he unzipped the fly on his trousers. His right hand and fingers became fully active. Parked at the cemetery, he satisfied his mind's fantasy. The only evidence left was a damp spot on his trousers.

May 1970, Cynthia Divorced

During Cynthia's first pregnancy, she acquired refined symmetry and looked positively ravishing. Just before the final divorce date, Cynthia gave birth to a beautiful blonde girl in May. Larry and Cynthia agreed on the name Rebecca. Their divorce became final later that month.

Hardy and his wife divorced a year later.

"I'll never marry again," he swore.

CHAPTER 4

Squeaky Hinges

Summer 1970, The Apartment

After Cynthia's divorce concluded, Put Put and her mother invited her and Baby Rebecca to move in with them. The child support payment allotted by the court provided for both their needs amply, with Cynthia doing away with a housing expense. The provided conveniences of living at home also gave her the luxurious time to refocus on herself, sewing new clothes, tanning, and exercising by swimming with Aunt Natty. Cynthia visited her aunt almost daily, bringing Baby Rebecca with her all summer. This warm afternoon Cynthia walked lazily up to Natty's apartment after her swim in the lake. She changed from her sport swimming suit, putting on a gauzy orange cover-up. Then she settled back on to Natty's white wicker divan out on the porch with Rebecca propped on pillows by her. Breezes from the lake glided through the screens to cool them.

"Darlink," Aunt Natty said to Cynthia, walking out on to the porch. "I don't know if you visit me so often because you enjoy my company more now that you are older, or if you simply need to get away from my dear brother. I certainly couldn't blame you for that either. I've a wonderful idea. I've been thinking. Why don't you move in here with Baby." Natty graciously offered her this opportunity while handing her a glass of Chardonnay. "I'm back and forth to

Alaska. There is plenty of room for me, too, when I come. I think it'll maybe afford you a little more privacy than living at Put Put's. You'd be right upstairs from Reginald if you needed help with anything." Natty set her own wineglass on the cream marble-top table next to her favorite white wicker chair with the cushion recovered in a brilliant pink and green floral Lilly fabric.

"Oh, Natty, what a marvelous gesture. Thank you. How kind you are. I'd really appreciate that. How can I thank you enough?" Cynthia accepted without hesitation. She had hoped for this offer from Aunt Natty.

"No need to thank, darlink," Natty answered her and took a sip of her pinot grigio. She lighted a cigarette, content with having invited her niece to live in her apartment.

The opulently furnished apartment still remained tasteful in the old style. The master bedroom hosted a pink marble-top dresser with a matching lady's vanity. The Lodge, being built before the age of closets, had a hand-carved cherrywood armoire that matched the four-poster bed. Some furnishings came from Golden Bounty, and some Natty commissioned from local artisans to complement specific furniture pieces. After Cynthia moved in, she transformed the sunroom off the dining room, with its warm southern exposure, into Baby Rebecca's nursery. She shopped sales and creatively redecorated it, turning the wallpaper sideways in pink and purple forget-me-not flowers with a lush dusty blue background. She sewed curtains of the same blue hue. The heirloom carved oak baby bed, originally belonging to Grandmother Parkton, was built so that it could collapse and be portable, unusual for its time. Cynthia assumed it must be worth some money.

At summer's end, Natty departed for Alaska. Cynthia continued to comfortably reside in the apartment with Baby Rebecca. Tonight she sat up on one elbow in the gigantic four-poster bed. Cynthia tilted her head a little to the left side to listen and focused her eyes toward the doorway like a golden retriever. She tried to hear the squeaky hinges. She did not hear them.

"Not yet," she said. Again she listened, adjusting the V in her pastel lime silk nightie so it matched the crevice between her breasts.

Reginald's so late tonight, she thought, pondering why The Lodge cocktail lounge would be busy on a chilly fall Wednesday night.

The glowing embers from the dying fire in the fireplace beautifully illuminated its keystone message "Where friends meet hearts warm." Downstairs Reginald finished cleaning up The Lodge cocktail lounge after he let the other help go. He walked around to the customer side of the bar and sat down on a comfortable stool. He lighted a cigarette and addressed his six-ounce glass of Korbel brandy. He called it "getting a base going." Quiet minutes passed. Relaxed now, he started up the staircase that rose beside the fireplace to the second-floor landing with the balance of his drink. He pushed the apartment door open with his free hand and looked disdainfully down at the squeaky hinges.

"Damn it! I need to oil those things one of these days," he muttered.

Cynthia cocked her head when she heard the hinges. She put down the cheap novel she had been reading and fluffed her silky, sunny blonde hair.

*****

Cynthia's mother, Alice, finally became exhausted by Put Put's carryings on and divorced him that fall. Put Put Parkton, in his new freedom, took up with a divorcee, a former executive's wife of the washing machine manufacturing plant in Belmont. They united themselves in common law marriage. One of the divorcee's children, Patty, a pretty seventeen-year-old blonde girl with substantial breasts, lived with Put Put and her mother at his house at The Lake. She was a senior in high school. With the winter population of The Lake numbering less than a thousand people, small school classes existed. Cynthia's class had graduated only fourteen students. Everyone knew everyone. Children became friends or not friends, depending on the status of the parents. Family background, old family money, social standings, and the parents' occupation all overtly determined the children's associations in the small-town environment.

Cynthia was glad she had learned to sew. She wanted to dress well, always looking chic, to associate with the wealthier summer people, which she strived to be part of. She did achieve this with her marriage to Larry Young. She remained detached from the small-town setting during her high school years with the exception of her friendship with Billy Benwolfski. She always appreciated his super-quick mind sparked with humor. He never failed to make her and everyone laugh, like his storytelling of Put Put and Slow Knocker at Noble's last summer.

Thus Cynthia's former upperclassman and schoolmate, Billy Benwolfski, and she became good friends all through their young lives. Billy also became an early admirer of Put Put and his turtle trapping, goose, duck, and deer hunting understudy. Billy spent one year at the nearby state college. Back at The Lake, he lived at his grandfather's cottage again. He loved his life. He became involved with Put Put's inventions, visiting his house frequently. The pretty Patty girl with blonde hair and overly ample breasts did not escape his eyes.

Fall 1970, Toby Marky

Billy encouraged his best friend, Toby Marky, his college room-mate for one year, to visit often from Port Michigan. Toby would accompany Billy on his visits to Put Put's house. He learned a great deal about the wildlife and surrounding areas of The Lake. Toby, like Billy, thoroughly enjoyed Put Put's stories about the Winnebago Indians of The Lake. He admired Put Put's creative intelligence and found the inventions Put Put tried to market fascinating.

During Toby's visit at the end of deer hunting season in November, Cynthia and Baby Rebecca stopped in to visit Put Put on Sunday. She didn't expect to find Billy there, and this good-looking guy with him too. She wore a short herringbone tweed wool skirt and jacket she sewed herself. Her superior sewing skills allowed her to don the latest styles, made to fit only her at an inexpensive price. She wore the jacket opened despite the cold weather. She held Baby

Rebecca lovingly in the crook of her left arm. The way she held Baby Rebecca revealed through her translucent silk blouse the tan line at the top of her breasts, which she still remarkably maintained from the summer. Rubbing golden peanut oil into her skin revitalized the sun-kissed color. Her long, slender legs extended below the hem of her short wool skirt in semitransparent hose, which matched the color of her blouse.

"Billy, hi. I didn't expect to find you here."

"Wow. Hi, Cynthia," Billy said, surprised to see her too. "Haven't seen you since summer. This is my roomie from when I went to college, Toby Marky."

"Hello," she said.

"We just stopped in here to celebrate after hunting with Put Put. I shot a buck. Ten points. Pretty damn good, wouldn't you say? Actually, I shot it last night before hunting started out the truck window and hid it in the barn until this morning to register it," he said. Everyone laughed. Then he motioned to Toby. "This is Cynthia. She's Put Put's daughter."

"Howdy," he said, tongue-tied by her beauty.

Billy definitely did not preplan any matchmaking. In fact, an idea of Toby and Cynthia never occurred to him. However, as soon as he caught Toby's obvious quick response to Cynthia, Billy's thoughts opened to a possible comfortable double-dating situation.

Later, Toby asked Billy, "What's the chances for me to see Cynthia again?"

"I'll fix it. Leave it to me," Billy said, grinning. "Why don't you see what you can do about coming up next weekend even though deer season is over? Hey, buddy, I just bet, by playing cupid for you, Sally will finally let Patty go out with me, with Cynthia along."

Toby gave him a friendly affirmative punch in the arm. They both laughed, amused by their own cleverness.

Billy stopped by The Lodge on Tuesday night, his night off from Noble's.

"Hi, Reginald, how's it going?" Billy asked, leaning on the empty bar.

"Going slow, but what do you expect for the end of November? It'll pick up now with some Christmas parties."

"Guess I'll have a beer or two. Is Cynthia upstairs?" Billy asked. "I wanted to say hi, and talk to her for a minute."

"Yeah, she's up there. Go up. Tell her I'll be done early tonight, okay? I'll get your Miller and have a drink with you. Silverfox isn't around tonight," Reginald replied.

"You should grease those squeaky hinges on that entrance door to the suite up there when it's so slow. Give you something to do," Billy joked with him. "They're worse than fingernails on a chalkboard, and louder."

The following Saturday, Cynthia, with Baby Rebecca, dropped in at Put Put's at five o'clock as Billy suggested. Put Put, his partner Sally, Patty, Billy, and Toby all sat around the kitchen table, playing crazy eights and drinking beer.

"Remember my friend Toby? He loves this place. He's back again this weekend," Billy said to Cynthia.

"I asked Billy what you liked to drink, just in case you stopped in again at your dad's," Toby butted in, standing up to offer her his chair. "I brought a bottle of Kendall Chardonnay from Port Michigan. Would you care for a glass?" Patty got up and scrambled for a wineglass.

"That would be very nice, thank you. Hi, everyone." She sat down in the chair that Toby offered her. "I like the shirt you're wearing, Toby. Where did you ever find something like that with the Labrador dogs in it?" Cynthia asked.

"I'm the manager of the men's department at Helen of Troy. It's the highest-quality department store in Port Michigan," Toby said, beaming from the compliment. He handed her a glass of Chardonnay and then pulled up another chair next to her.

"Yes, yes, I've heard a lot about Helen of Troy," she said. "Lots of the summer people here at The Lake shop there."

"Yeah, he stuck out college and actually got a degree in business. Right, Toby?" Billy volunteered.

"You have a degree in business and are manager of the men's department at Helen of Troy's? I'm very impressed, Toby." She smiled at him. Giving him eye contact, she took a sip of her wine. "What nice-tasting wine, and so thoughtful of you. Thank you."

*****

Toby called Cynthia the following Wednesday afternoon.

"I can get away from work to come up to The Lake just for Friday night. Billy said the fish fry is really good at Mid Point. We could go together with Billy and Patty, if you'd like to go. I guess Sally will let Patty go if you're along too. I think Billy really wants to go out with her."

"I'd be delighted, Toby," she answered.

"Really? That's just swell," he said. "I'll see you Friday then. Billy will tell me the arrangements."

"Yes, see you then. Thank you. I'm looking forward to it, Toby."

With winter approaching, Baby Rebecca, Reginald, and the reading of cheap paperback novels had become her total life. A chance for something else to do suited her just fine.

"Hello?" Sally answered.

"Hi. It's Cynthia. I'm calling because I'm wondering if you and Dad could possibly take care of Rebecca if I go out with Patty, Billy, and his friend for fish Friday night up at Mid Point? Will you let Patty go?" Cynthia asked Sally, this being the first time Cynthia ever asked for a babysitting favor.

"Sure, that's okay. I don't see any reason not to. Patty can go, too, with you along. I'll tell Put Put. He'll agree to watch Rebecca for a while with me. She's such a good girl."

When she heard the squeaky hinges that night, she went to sit at the round dining table with Reginald when he came in.

"Natty's cheap white wine is terrible," she began, setting her glass down.

"You know I can't bring you a decent wine up from the bar when Silverfox is around," he said, taking a sip of his Meyers and Tab he smuggled from the bar.

"When I stopped at Dad's Friday, a friend of Billy's, Toby, was there. I'd met him before at Dad's. He brought a whole bottle of expensive Chardonnay for me in case I'd be there."

"You're so lucky," Reginald said and lighted a cigarette.

"He called me today. He asked me to go to Mid Point for fish with him, Billy, and Patty, Friday. I said I'd go, right away. It'll give me a chance to get out for a change. Plus, you never have any money to take me anyplace, ever, when you're off."

Reginald simply took a chug of his cocktail and didn't bother to answer her.

Summer 1971, Hardy's Visit

As spring arrived in 1971, Reginald became aware that his weekend time with Cynthia somewhat lessened. By summer, he became acutely aware that his weekends with Cynthia disappeared altogether.

August came with Hardy's annual visit. Since he had already experienced Cynthia being with Toby the whole first weekend after he arrived, Hardy figured he and Reginald should get out a little after Reginald closed the bar.

When Hardy came from Connecticut, he always brought his daughter, Amber. He planted her at his ex-in-law's for most of the time, except for luncheon dates with him. The grandparents loved it. Hardy rented a cottage for a week. He would be footloose and fancy-free after depositing his daughter safely away. If he could possibly stay longer, he would crash at Connie's cottage. He wanted no schedule when on vacation away from his First National Alden Bank of Connecticut. He became the president after his father passed last January, with his younger brother, Mitchell, second in command.

"Let's play it by ear" became his favorite line when he vacationed at The Lake.

At The Lodge, Hardy sat across the bar from Reginald on Friday night.

"Well, my week at the rental cottage is up tomorrow," Hardy commented with his cigarette almost singeing his eyebrows as he drank his JB and water. "I don't know if I should stay a little longer or not. I didn't see Cynthia except for two nights. God, she looked marvelous, when we were here last night, didn't she, Reginald," he stated, rather than asking an opinion. He pushed his glass forward for a refill. He smiled to himself. She wore a creamy brown sundress without a back, almost the same color as her golden tan. The first glances he took of her in that ensemble made him visualize her as a naked goddess, a delightful thought indeed.

"God, she looked spectacular," he repeated aloud again and smiled. "Who is this Toby guy that Billy Benwolfski dragged up here from Port Michigan? He's even here in the middle of the week. He drove up from Port Michigan special for Mexican night at Mid Point, Wednesday night. I met him."

"Yeah, he does that now once in a while too. It started out just being a night on the weekend," Reginald glumly interjected, rubbing his nose.

"Cynthia and the other three seemed to be having a lot of fun," Hardy continued. "She was doing slammers. That Patty girl Billy is with probably isn't old enough to be drinking in there. But who cares? He's really hooked on her. She's cute with big boobs. That Toby guy couldn't keep his eyes off Cynthia or his hands either. Ah, Cynthia. God, what a beauty," Hardy concluded wistfully.

Reginald tried to listen while tending to other customers and the waitresses' drink orders. True enough, Reginald knew Cynthia did not have time for him right now. At least Hardy got to spend a couple of days and nights with her and baby Rebecca during his stay.

The bar action slowed. "Hardy, I know when that Toby guy is around because I can always hear those damn squeaky hinges up there. I never did oil them. It's a regular weekend fling," Reginald said. "Don't know much about the guy. Guess he and Billy were room-mates at college. He's nothing special. Works selling men's clothes in some big department store in Port Michigan," Reginald answered.

"So that's why he dresses like he has money," Hardy mused.

"Yeah, suppose so. She's with him every Friday, Saturday, and Sunday. That I do know. He brings her clothes from that department store. She always makes a point of telling me. I think they're ugly," Reginald volunteered, irritated.

"Guess I'll stay through Monday night then and go back Tuesday. See her Monday night. Crash at Connie's this weekend. Maybe go out on her pontoon. Want to hit the hot spots after you're done here?" Hardy asked.

"You mean the only hot spot." Reginald smirked and laughed. "Sure, ten o'clock or so. Maybe we'll get lucky with something."

"I'll go up to Mid Point now and see what's up there. See ya later," Hardy said, then laughed too.

*****

Hardy walked into the fish fry and instantly spotted Cynthia at the bar with Toby, Billy, and Patty.

"Shit," he grumbled to himself. "Do I have to meet the guy again?" He crossed the crowded barroom to stand at the bar between Cynthia and Billy, requiring Cynthia's immediate attention to be turned away from Toby seated on her other side.

"JB and water?" asked Danny Boy, the owner from behind the bar. He recognized Hardy immediately.

"Gee, yes, thanks, Dan." Hardy nodded and lighted a cigarette, gazing at Cynthia. She looked ravishing, he thought, even though the outfit she wore was definitely not his choice. The black and white small-checked sundress's ample shoulder straps covered way too much of her flaxen tan. The ensemble's style made it apparent that she wore underwear. Hardy cringed at the thought. Black sandals with little white bows and a black tie in her blonde hair completed the look. *Reginald's right*, he thought, *ugly*. He looked directly into her eyes and said, "I'm staying through Monday night. I'd like to take you to Noble's my last night here, Cynthia."

"I'll have to see if Dad and Sally will take care of Rebecca." She smiled, gazing back into his eyes, then added coyly, "Because they've been watching her quite a bit already this weekend while Toby's here."

Hardy felt like a bucket of cold water was dumped on his head. He took a chug of his JB and water and a drag off his cigarette. He exhaled the smoke slowly.

"Try for Monday," Hardy said. He finished his JB and water. "I've barely seen you since I came this time."

"Another, Hardy?" the owner asked from his good listening position behind the bar.

"No, thanks," he said. "Going to meet Reginald and see what we can drum up later tonight. Probably see you over at Noble's, Billy," Hardy said with a friendly grin.

"Who cares what you drum up as long she can walk and breathe," Billy chimed in, chuckling. The owner laughed too. Cynthia made eye contact through a side glance with her first cousin. She did not laugh.

Hardy addressed the four at the bar. "Well, Reginald and I'll probably be at Noble's if you all swing in there, but we're going to play it by ear. Maybe we'll see you later." He left some money on the bar.

"At least I'll be there for sure," Billy said as a joke, "working."

Hardy and Cynthia exchanged another glance.

*****

Monday came. Cynthia talked with her father.

"Sure, we'll babysit Rebecca while Hardy takes you to Noble's for dinner," Put Put said. "I think it's just great you're still such good friends with your cousin."

At five o'clock, the forever-tan Cynthia came down the stairs at The Lodge wearing a pink-gauze pant ensemble. The halter top tied around the back of her neck and at the back of her waist. Obviously not wearing a bra, she noticeably oozed with visual sexual allure. Reginald began to register that she always appeared to be without underwear when he would see her with Hardy. *It must be a coincidence,* he thought and chuckled to himself about his observations, rubbing his nose. She looked like she just stepped out of a Frederick's of Hollywood catalog. Hardy sat waiting for her at the bar.

"Would you like a champagne or wine here, or are we right on to Noble's?" Hardy asked, standing up and pushing up his glasses.

"Hi, Hardy, and Reginald." She kissed Hardy on the cheek. He drew her close. "We can go to Noble's and have a drink there. Is that okay?" Cynthia asked, pulling away.

"Great, that's great. Okay, my chariot awaits you, Princess. Later, Reginald,"

Cynthia ordered a succulent dinner at Noble's. It began with oysters Rockefeller on the half shell, followed by lobster thermidor. Hardy reveled in her presence. He delighted in all the money he could spend on her.

After dinner, they collected Baby Rebecca from Put Put's. The three returned to The Lodge. Cynthia and Rebecca left the bar almost immediately after saying goodbye to Hardy, issuing him a lingering goodbye kiss on the mouth. Reginald closed his eyes to it. She disappeared up the staircase, leaving Hardy at the bar with Reginald. Hardy sat with his JB and water and lighted a cigarette. Behind him the staircase ascended beside the fireplace to Cynthia's door. Reginald glanced at Hardy's package on the bar in a plain brown wrapper. He remembered when he ordered things that arrived in plain brown wrappers. He shook his head, nervously running his hand over his nose.

"It is my imagination," he mumbled to himself.

The last two customers besides Hardy left the bar. The room now became empty and quiet, except for the clicking of the Hamm's beer light.

"Well," Hardy said, taking a slow drag on his cigarette. "I'm going to be sliding out."

"Yeah, I'm heading out soon too," replied Reginald, preoccupied. "I need to grab the keys from the back room to close up."

Not even a minute passed before Reginald stepped back into the bar. To his surprise, Hardy was gone. Unusual for Hardy, his drink remained half full. The package no longer lay on the bar. Then Reginald's ears alertly honed in on the top of staircase. His mouth dropped ajar. He heard those squeaky hinges.

CHAPTER 5

Number Two

September 1971, Pregnant

Cynthia gripped the toilet bowl and vomited into it again, as she had yesterday morning.

"Oh, shit. Damn," she sputtered. "I just can't be. God, I feel terrible."

The calendar page showed September. With Hardy there in August and Toby's continuing attention, she lost track of marking the calendar for her periods. After she recovered from this round of morning sickness, she walked to Rebecca's crib to lift her out. Rebecca, a year and three months old now, made happy *goos* and gurgles as Cynthia carried her to the cherrywood high chair by the carved oak dining table overlooking The Lake. Cynthia snapped the calendar off the wall and threw it down on the table with firm determination. Carefully she analyzed the days. She counted and marked off her ovulation time frame in July.

"Ten, seven, eleven, well, that erases Reginald from the picture," she said, throwing her pencil down on the table. "I put him on the back burner before the Fourth of July weekend started. That's when Toby began bringing me those cute outfits from Helen of Troy. He must have used his employee discount after he figured out I especially liked pink. He probably thought bringing me the provocative pink underpants would make it easier for him to pry them off.

"Okay," Cynthia said to Rebecca. "Having Toby's baby wouldn't be the worst thing in the world, now, would it? He has a decent job, he's never been married, no baggage or strings, good-looking, and he's genuinely in love with me."

"Goo, goo," Rebecca responded.

Cynthia picked up the pencil and tapped the table, thinking. She also knew he purchased a modest home in a lovely suburb of Port Michigan. Lucky for Toby he showed a good work history with little debt in his young life. The pencil point broke off.

"Hmm," she said to Rebecca. "We'll ask Aunt Natty if she'd give us some antique furnishings to take with us from The Lodge. And you know what else, Rebecca? Connie lives there. That's a plus. But Reginald—why, oh why not Reginald?" she implored Rebecca, pausing as if she expected an answer. She affectionately ruffled Rebecca's curly blonde hair. "It's mid-September," Cynthia rattled on. "Winter will be coming. Maybe it's time for us to leave The Lake."

Rebecca bounced in her high chair, shaking her bunny rattle.

That afternoon Reginald came by for his usual visit before he opened The Lodge bar downstairs. He plunked down at the dining room table.

"What's the calendar here for?" he asked, pushing it aside with his ashtray.

"Reginald, I'm pregnant," she declared.

He smoked his cigarette. Fixing his eyes on her, he nervously rubbed his mouth and nose.

"Did you hear what I said? I said I'm pregnant."

"Yeah, yeah," he mumbled. "I heard. What do you want me to do?"

"I'm going to marry Toby," she stated.

Reginald choked on his own cigarette smoke. He stared at her while vigorously rubbing his hand over his mouth and nose again.

"Well, I know it's his baby," she volunteered.

"How do you know that?" he accused.

"I figured it out by the dates. It's his," she confirmed.

"Why not marry me?" he blurted.

"Because you know you don't have a decent job. We both know how much money tending bar here at The Lodge pays. You tinker, tinker, tinker on those old boats with Billy all the time, but that doesn't bring in any money either. You should have used your GI bill and finished college when you came back from Vietnam. You're so smart, Reginald. You're not doing anything with your brains. Rebecca needs security although Larry never misses his support payments. I need to be taken care of too. The child support and my alimony stipend doesn't go far, you know." She added after a pensive pause, "Plus, there's going to be a new baby, I must have sufficient money for my life."

"You look ravishing sitting there ruining my life. So what do you want me to do? Go to Belmont and work in the factory?" he retorted on the defense.

"No, no, I don't really want that." She sighed and looked down. "Hardy said he would try to come out here toward the end of this month for his birthday. I'll tell him then."

"What's so important about telling him?" Reginald rubbed out his cigarette.

She did not answer.

*****

Hardy did plan to get away to The Lake at the end of September. Having relatives at The Lake generated a good excuse at the bank to visit them for his birthday. Being at The Lake for the first time after Labor Day excited Hardy.

Above all, Hardy envisioned his birthday dinner at The Lodge with his princess, Cynthia. "Ah." He sighed, fantasizing. For his birthday, she would descend the staircase looking like The Lake goddess.

He made his reservation and called Connie on the phone. "My flight will get into Port Mich at three-fifteen Friday afternoon," he said to her. "How would it work for with your schedule to pick me up and drive me to The Lake? I'll arrange with Billy to bring my car to the motel."

"Let's see. Yeah, I can figure it out for this Friday. I've wanted to go up there anyway. It's been since Labor Day weekend. This is the perfect excuse," Connie answered.

After the two-hour drive on Friday from Port Michigan to The Lake, Hardy checked in at his reserved motel room located in the four downtown blocks of Monapacataca. Then he drove the three miles over to The Lodge. Reginald had just opened up The Lodge bar, hoping for some predinner cocktail business when he saw Hardy walking in.

"Hardy," Reginald genuinely greeted him, glad to see him again. "I've someone to talk to at the bar now." He gestured toward the empty bar. They laughed and shook hands. "Heard you're coming. It's a birthday thing? Usual?" Reginald talked as he mixed Hardy's JB and water. He rested his cigarette in the same ashtray as Hardy's. "Happy birthday, on me," Reginald exclaimed, placing Hardy's cocktail on the bar.

"Let me get you one." Hardy pointed at the Meyer's bottle.

"Sure." Reginald smiled. "Silverfox already has been around. He won't be back tonight. There's not enough business. It's still too early for my base of Korbel brandy. I'll have a Sapphire gin martini instead."

"The locals are right. It's sure quiet. But I like the half price on the motel room," Hardy said.

"Yeah. After Labor Day, the switch is turned off. All the summer people disappear back to the shitties. School starts. Tranquility reigns again." Reginald paused when he saw Hardy set down a small package on the bar in a plain brown wrapper. He did a double take. It seemed like déjà vu. Hardy did not notice.

"Going to sneak up and see Cynthia for a minute. She's expecting me," he told Reginald. He put out his cigarette and took a quick chug. "I'll just let my drink sit here."

"Don't worry. It'll be here," Reginald answered back.

Hardy turned and hastily walked toward the staircase.

"Didn't finish his drink and all wound up," Reginald said. He chuckled to himself. "Must be jet lag or something." For a second he pondered the package, now gone from the bar. He remembered the last time he saw Hardy with a package at the bar on his last visit. Hardy and the package disappeared then too. "Crazy," he declared out loud, rubbing his nose.

Ten minutes later Hardy returned down the stairs. He plunked down comfortably on a barstool opposite Reginald.

"Yeah, for my birthday, we're going to have dinner right here at The Lodge tomorrow night. Tonight that Toby guy is coming up from the city. Hasn't changed, has it, Reginald? Anyway, Saturday night will be great, great. Cynthia can bring Rebecca with her. We'll go back upstairs to visit for a while afterwards. Guess I'll make reservations now. Tonight I'll meet up with Connie later at Noble's. You'll probably be done early? Right?" His excitement gushed out from him.

"Don't think you'll need reservations. No people." Reginald laughed as he watched Hardy head toward the gal with the reservation book. By Hardy's enthusiasm, Reginald assumed Cynthia did not drop the big one on him yet. She must be waiting until after dinner tomorrow night. Well, he pondered, it would be her style to wait until after the little birthday dinner to tell him.

"Boy oh boy, especially the part about her planning to marry Toby Marky..." Reginald mumbled to himself. "Boy, my guts tell me Hardy sure has no use for Cynthia's boyfriend." Reginald ran his hand over his nose again and shook his head.

Hardy returned to the bar. "All set for tomorrow night. Think I'll head to Mid Point before Noble's. Is Billy tending bar at Noble's?"

"Think so, yeah. So you'll be there around ten?" Reginald asked, glad for something to do.

"Yeah, probably. Let's play it by ear."

*****

The next day late in the afternoon, Reginald opened The Lodge bar. The sun would be setting before 6:30 p.m. this time of the year, making the shortening of each day so very apparent. This astronomical fact could depress a person.

Hardy strolled in, being the very first customer.

"Hey, Hardy. What have you been up to today? Look pretty spiffy." Reginald shook his hand and then poured Hardy's usual JB and water. Hardy had donned his best black Brooks Brothers suit with a crisp pink shirt and a distinctive berry pink tie for his birthday dinner at The Lodge with Cynthia. His gold tie clasp glistened with bold initials ANB, standing for Alden's National Bank.

"Well, nobody at Noble's last night, that's for sure. Well, you, Connie, and me, and we're the important people. Right? Have one," Hardy told Reginald. "Not even Billy tending bar last night. Where's Billy? Say, I need to use the telephone. It's a big football weekend, both college and pros."

"Sure. Calm down, man. Have a sip of your drink. You're bouncing around like you're on drugs or something. To answer your first question, I heard Billy is down in Port Michigan cleaning out some estate for his mother, and I'll take a straight Coke, thanks. It's too early. Silverfox will be around tonight."

Hardy paid no attention, his mind already imagining the dinner with Cynthia, dreaming of how she would look tonight. He emptied his drink. Reginald refilled it without asking. "Phone's up at the reception desk. Hasn't moved since you used it the last time." Reginald rubbed his nose. *He must have a bookie,* Reginald thought.

"Okay, I'll be right back," Hardy said.

Five minutes later, he returned to the bar and settled down onto a stool.

"It's amazing how early the sun goes down into The Lake this time of year, isn't it, Reginald?" Hardy reflected while dreamily gazing out at the setting sun over the west end of The Lake. "This shore sure is the best." He sighed, taking a drag on his cigarette. "The way the setting sun shimmers in through the windows is just, well, it's just splendid. Isn't it?" Hardy sighed again, sipping his fresh JB and water.

"Yeah, yeah," Reginald agreed, glancing at him quizzically, momentarily wondering about this unseen side of Hardy. He stepped away from Hardy and the bar, gazing at the sun fading slowly into The Lake. The golden flush of sunset turned to crimson, and then purple. The grays followed. These forerunners of the night changed the entire landscape. Reginald watched with pensive eyes. The leaves on the trees dyed in yellows and reds last week now lay brown on the ground. The autumn wind wailed through the trees as though they mourned their coming fate. Reginald saw sadness in the whole aspect of nature tonight. As he gazed through the window, the glass did not reflect Reginald's face as a cheerful one.

"Cynthia, why can't it be me?" Reginald murmured, still turned toward the window. "It'll always be Cynthia, the love of my life." Hardy did not hear him. "If she won't marry me, I'll go unmarried to the grave." His lips trembled with a long-drawn, bitter sob. Startled by the sound of her coming down the staircase, he turned back from the window with contempt for his own weakness, his love for her.

Cynthia descended the stairs holding Rebecca, taking one slow step at a time. Cynthia wore a crimson, almost purple, long-sleeved floor-length dress that shimmered softly in the restaurant's golden lights. She lowered a drape in the drop of the bodice to reveal the tan line on her ample breasts. The dress gave her an ambiance glowing with beauty, yet innocence. Reginald watched the love of his life and Hardy's goddess descend from the kingdom of heaven. Hardy's face beamed as melon pink as his tie.

The colors in the dress pitifully reminded Reginald of the setting sun he just watched through the bar window. Cynthia's face showed an embracing smile for both men.

"Hardy, if they have a table ready for us, we should sit right down. It would be easier with Rebecca."

"Sure, sure," he agreed quickly, eager to please. He immediately hurried to ask the hostess.

Cynthia raised and tilted her beautiful head toward Reginald. "Haven't told him yet," she whispered. "We'll have a pleasant dinner first. Hardy isn't going to like hearing I'm pregnant, especially when I'm sure it's Toby's and I intend to marry him."

"Do you think I liked hearing it?" Reginald blurted out.

"Table is all ready." Hardy bounded back, returning to Cynthia's side at the bar. He leaned over to put his cigarette out in the bar ashtray and chugged the rest of his JB water. "Later." Hardy nodded toward Reginald.

The Lodge's polished dining room's solid carved cherrywood tables and chairs gleamed in the Queen Anne style. The seats, covered in royal blue linen, invited guests to immediate comfort. The waitresses' wore floor-length dresses and white gloves. A plump waitress in a navy blue dress and white collar welcomed them. She led them to their table. A matching child's carved cherrywood high chair, similar to the one in Natty's apartment, had been positioned already at the table. After seating them, the waitress offered them menus.

"Would you care for a beverage from the bar to start your dinner this evening?" the waitress inquired.

"JB and water. Cynthia?"

"A glass of Chardonnay would be nice." She smiled. Her mind briefly fast-forwarded to telling Hardy the news.

Two minutes later the waitress brought their drinks and began to take their dinner orders.

"Mam, I'll start with you, please."

"I'd like the Caesar salad. I just love it when Mr. Silverfox prepares it tableside. He's here this evening, isn't he?"

"Yes, he's here."

"Wonderful. The Caesar salad will be all for me. What is the soup, please?" Cynthia questioned.

"Soupe au pistou or vichyssoise."

"Let's see, I think the soupe au pistou will be delicious for Rebecca. Water wafers on the side, please. Nothing else." Again she smiled at Hardy.

"And you, sir?"

"Steak Diane, and what's the vegetable?" He lighted a cigarette and rested it in the ashtray.

"A julienned carrots medley, sir."

"No, thank you, just a salad with vinegar and oil," he replied.

How boring and drab, the waitress thought.

"Would you care for a soup this evening to begin your meal, sir?" she asked.

"Yes, thank you very much, the vichyssoise."

"I'll start the dinners all at the same time if that is okay. Thank you," the waitress said and retreated from the table.

Hardy softly spoke to Cynthia. "I don't see that I can get out here again until possibly Winter Festival time. That may be a good time to do a getaway," he stated, looking at her with a masterful gaze from behind his black horn-rimmed glasses.

"It's so bleak in January at Winter Festival time, Hardy. Maybe later in the season after the Kentucky Derby is over for you. Maybe in spring for a long weekend and still your usual time in August, so we could do Rebecca's and Amber's birthday celebrations together August?" She entered the words for his thought. She did not want him to see her pregnant this winter.

Dinner concluded. The time came to go upstairs to the apartment. Hardy escorted them up the stairs. Cynthia mixed him a JB and water and handed it to him. She set an ashtray on the end table. He leaned back comfortably on Natty's eight-foot-long black leather sofa, admiring the clean and well-preserved mahogany adornment. Cynthia busied herself putting Rebecca to bed. The inevitable time came. She sat down in the matching chair next to Hardy.

"Hardy, I need to talk with you about something," she nervously began.

"Hmm…" He smiled at her warmly.

Then she flung herself at his knees. She raised her large blue eyes toward Hardy's face and took his pale white hands and kissed them.

"Hardy, I'm pregnant with Toby's baby," she murmured.

Harden rose to his feet, pacing with quick, impatient steps. His eyes opened behind his black-rimmed glasses in fiery astonishment. His face turned whiter than white. His lips became colorless.

"Toby, Toby," he repeated the name with a demonstrative, disdained voice. "You're pregnant? From Toby Marky?" interrogated Hardy. "It's impossible."

"Yes, it's Toby's, without a doubt," she replied quietly, beautiful and nervous.

"For heaven sake, I'll help you. It's incredible. You must let me help you. I'll do everything I can," he cried eagerly. "You certainly can't think of having this baby," he promptly continued. Cynthia remained on her knees trembling. Harden slid down on his knees by his cousin's side. "My darling," mastering his feelings. "I shouldn't have suggested to you to undertake such a thing as an abortion. Can you ever forgive me?"

She kissed him. "You're thinking it all for the best," she said.

"We'll arrange together what's better to be done," he interjected.

"I'm going to have the baby, and marry Toby," she quietly, but definitely, said.

Hardy's time, limited by the bank in Connecticut, forced him to adhere to his tight schedule and leave Monday morning as planned.

Monday afternoon Reginald trudged up the outside stairs to Natty's apartment at the time he would every day before setting up the bar downstairs. Mr. Silverfox decided not to open The Lodge bar and restaurant any longer during the off season this fall and winter on Monday and Tuesday. On these days the inside stairs could not be used. He opened the door to the apartment from the outside and shuffled over to sit down at the round oak table. Surprised to find the room quiet, he called Cynthia's name.

"Cynthia, you here?" he called. He heard her rustling about in her bedroom.

"Yes, I am. I'll be right out. I took a little rest," she answered back.

She entered the room tying her sheer French pink provocative silk robe draped around her in the front. The back flowed free. Fuzzy precocious pink slippers warmed her feet.

"I took advantage of Rebecca's rest time to take a nap myself," she said, sitting down.

"What are you doing sleeping during the middle of the afternoon?" he asked, lighting a cigarette, and felt himself getting hard just looking at her.

"I'm pregnant, remember? I needed to take little naps the first months with Rebecca too," she said. "I told Hardy everything. He suggested an abortion at first. But we both knew that wasn't right. So I'm still going to marry Toby."

"Does the lucky bridegroom know yet?' Reginald threw in sarcastically.

"No, I'll tell him this Friday," she answered matter-of-factly.

November 1971, Married

The next weekend Reginald looked up from behind the bar with great interest when Toby Marky arrived and ascended the stairs. Reginald lighted a cigarette. He knew the staircase climb so well. He had already passed through that stage. Then Hardy had received the blow. *Well, this is the finale,* he thought. *I wonder what the hussy will do if he won't marry her.*

*****

Cynthia kissed Toby when he entered the apartment. "You made excellent time on your drive up from the city. How about a beer?"

He took the beer from her and sat down on the comfortable black leather sofa, ready to relax after the drive. She curled up next to him with a glass of Chardonnay. He barely took a sip of his beer before he heard Cynthia's unexpected announcement.

"Toby, I'm pregnant," she said. She watched him for his reaction. A quiet cloud hung over their heads. Then Toby stood up straight and resolute. He gathered Cynthia into his arms from the sofa.

"I should imagine, that I'll take my full share of responsibility," Toby spoke, looking into her blue eyes. "Nothing should part us. Will you be my wife, Cynthia?" he nobly asked. "I do love you, even more now with my baby."

She covered her face with her hands in relief, hiding her pained reaction to such loving words. Toby misread the gesture, thinking her comforted and appreciative. His love immediately grew deeper and stronger as he held her.

"Toby, let's elope," Cynthia said. "At least let's keep the baby a secret until after we're married."

"Let me think about it a little. I'm still really surprised." He guided her onto the sofa and plopped down next to her. He put his arm around her to draw her toward him. "How many months are you, sweetheart?"

"Since July," Cynthia said.

"Yes, probably sooner is better than later," Toby said. "A civil ceremony in Port Michigan might be the answer." He kissed her lightly on her rose-painted lips. "I'll see what I can find out on Monday. I'll call you after work on Monday with all the information I learn. Now let's just go up to Mid Point for fish. I'm starved," he said. "I think we need not dwell on it right now. Everything will be okay." He tried to lighten the tense mood. He gave her another hug for reassurance and took a chug of his beer still sitting on the side table next to him on the sofa.

She reached across him for her Chardonnay. She liked the change in the atmosphere, taking advantage of it immediately. "Well, I took Rebecca to Dad's earlier, and I'm ready to go," she said. She smiled and kissed him warmly. He liked that. *Yes, everything will be good with Cynthia as my wife,* he thought.

*****

Monday, Toby located a Judge Jacobson who would be available to perform the civil ceremony as soon as a week from the coming Friday in the afternoon. The judge did this on Fridays only. It would be in his chambers at the Port Michigan Courthouse at 3:00 p.m. His wife would fill the position of witness. Toby felt lucky to be able to schedule a time so quickly. He called Cynthia Monday night with the great news.

"Toby, I'm thrilled you could manage to arrange all this so fast. Oh, honey, you're super." Cynthia sighed with relief.

"I feel rather fortunate myself. When I come this Friday, be ready to bring here what you need for at least the nextweek. We'll come back here right away Saturday morning to my house."

"For Rebecca too," Cynthia said. "I will."

"Then next week we'll need to get the license and blood tests right away. I think I know a neighbor lady, Mrs. Watson, who will probably be okay with watching Rebecca when we need her to help us out. I need to talk with her yet. No one else will know until after, like we want," he said.

"Oh, Toby, thank you. I love you," she said. "I'll need to shop for my wedding dress, but I can bring Rebecca with me for that. I've taken her shopping with me before, lots of times."

"I'll figure it out so you can come with me to work at Helen and use my discount," Toby said. "Then come back with the car, and pick me up after I'm through for the day. After we're married, we'll go up to The Lake, with a U-Haul, to get the furniture you want."

"Oh, Toby, you think of everything," she said. *I'm so ridiculously lucky,* she thought.

*****

The Friday of the event came. Cynthia and Toby arrived at Judge Jacobson's chambers at two-thirty-five and waited for their turn at 3:00 p.m. Cynthia looked innocent wearing a pale pink sheath with white gloves and shoes. She held a small bouquet of white and pink roses. Toby wore a dark gray suit that he would also wear to work. After the brief legal ceremony, and "I pronounce you man and wife," the newlyweds drove to a Hilton near Toby's house for a late-afternoon dinner celebration between the two of them.

The next morning, Cynthia called Connie. "We didn't want to tell anyone until we were married," Cynthia said. "Anyway, one of the fun things about it is that I'll be able to see you more. Please don't tell anyone else yet."

"Of course, I won't. That's up to you. I must say, at the very least, I'm surprised. But if you say it's good, I'll go with good," Connie said. She sat down guessing the reason.

Sunday Toby and Cynthia discussed what she wanted to bring from The Lake to Toby's house in Port Michigan. They would rent the U-Haul for the following weekend to get the furniture moving done. She knew Toby would be talking to Billy, telling him, and asking him to help.

I must call Reginald, she thought. *I need to tell him.*

CHAPTER 6

Esther

Spring 1975, Esther

Esther, the product of Toby and Cynthia's union, proudly turned three in the spring of 1975. On this March day, she napped on the sofa along the wall. Her dark hair, so much like Toby's, spilled over the antique twinkle-pink pillows propped up to guard her while she slept. Toby always secretly hoped for a boy for his own namesake. But when Esther arrived, he loved her, loved her, and loved her. When he gazed into her chestnut brown eyes, he saw his own. He would hold her up in his arms high in the air. Cynthia insisted on a biblical name, so they decided on Esther. This name came from the book of Esther, a Persian name meaning "a star."

"My own little shining star," Toby would murmur, kissing Esther gently on her forehead.

Cynthia kept hoping Esther would help her to care more for Toby. But Toby's relentless attention for Esther sometimes left her overcome with jealousy.

*****

Billy's mother, with her job being the estate attorney's assistant in Belmont, needed a property and its contents liquidated in Port

Michigan. The deceased owner had committed suicide by slitting his wrists. While walking around his house, he sprayed the blood all over the windows. Knowing Billy needed the money, she gave him the job to do the clean-out work. Spring business still needed to begin again at The Lake. Noble's closed its doors Sunday night and did not reopen until Friday. This gave him four full days to work in Port Michigan. Billy started by hauling out the estate "merch" to sell at auction.

From the phone booth down at the corner near the house, Billy called Toby and Cynthia living in the suburbs.

"Yeah, I'll be back and forth for a few weeks. I'm hoping we can get together," Billy said to Toby.

"Oh yeah, great. We'll have you out for dinner. I'll talk to Cynthia and check my work schedule. Can you call back in a couple days?"

"Sure. I go back to The Lake on Thursday afternoons. I'll call you when I'm back next Monday. Talk to you then," Billy said.

Being in the phone booth already, Billy decided to call Reginald to ask him to come to the shitty.

"Yeah, help me clean. My mother will pay you."

"I only work Friday and Saturday nights at The Lodge right now. I could use the money too," Reginald said. *I'll probably be able to see Cynthia.* He pondered the idea, lighting a cigarette.

"Yeah, you can stay right here at the house," Billy encouraged him. "It's not far from the university. There're some bars. We can meet some college chicks."

Reginald did not hesitate. Silverfox said The Lodge would close altogether at the end of March. It would not open for the summer season again until May.

Reginald called Cynthia right away the next day to make plans to see her.

"What perfect timing, Reginald. My days are almost an open book. I'd love to see you, to be with you again. Rebecca is at school now all day. She's five in May. With Toby's promotion three months ago to management, he works some long days. I know Billy goes back to the Lake on Thursday. Call me back tomorrow, Reginald. I'll talk to Toby tonight."

"I just really need to get out once," Cynthia complained to Toby that night. "Can't you make a commitment to be home by two on Thursday for Rebecca so I can have the car and go visit Connie for dinner? Please, honey. I'll make kidney pie and take it with me for dinner. Connie likes it. I'll have your dinners all ready here too."

Cynthia knew Connie would be out of town for work on Thursday. There would be no chance of her calling.

"I say great about you taking the kidney pie with you," he said. He shook his head just thinking about having to eat one again. "But seriously, I do understand. I'll take care of it tomorrow for Thursday. I'll use a medical," he said. "Make your plans. It'll be good for you to get out and visit Connie."

Thursday she found the house in the city. The house and block looked run-down. This area around the university sounded loud, even noisy, compared to where Connie lived near Lake Michigan. Draped clothes hung over the windows of the house. She hesitated, pushing her car door with her foot. Then she saw Reginald stepping out of the front door. Her silly moment of hesitation vanished.

Inside the dusty living room in Reginald's waiting arms, the musty smell did not bother her. She even volunteered to help him clean for a while.

"Okay, great, good," Reginald said. They kissed again. "I'm going into the dining room to keep washing dried blood off windows." In the next room, Reginald's pulse raced from a hair-raising scare cleaning the aquarium when a bottom-feeder fish, still alive, jumped up at him from two inches of still-moist green slime blanketing the aquarium floor. Then Cynthia screamed from the adjacent room. "Oh my god, Cynthia! What, what?" he yelled and raced to her.

"Teeeeeeeeeeth. I found his teeth!" Cynthia grabbed hold of Reginald's arm. "Ish, teeth," she uttered. She dropped the cup containing the deceased's yellow, horrid dentures to the floor.

"Come on, let's go in the kitchen and have a drink. I bought some Chardonnay for you," he said, trying to regain composure. He kicked the cup aside with his foot. "I know you said you were bring-ing something special for dinner. The kitchen is all cleaned up. I put the package you brought for dinner in the refrigerator."

"Okay, good," she said. She nuzzled against him walking into the kitchen. "I'll heat up dinner in the oven,"

They sat together at the kitchen table, for a drink, while the kid-ney pie warmed. She got up to put plates and utensils on the table. She brought the pie from the oven. Reginald put out his cigarette and contemplated her flowered darling pink and purple girly dress. *A typical Toby dress,* Reginald dismally thought. *It fits with kidney pie.*

"I can't eat this," he grumbled.

"Well, it's my grandmother's recipe from The Lodge," she returned, open-eyed. "Guests always raved about it. They declared that a restaurant offering kidneys prepared to perfection meant every item on the menu to be excellent, Reginald."

"I don't care, it's awful. I won't eat this. It's just a big, old, round thing chopped up once or twice just sitting there. I've eaten it when your dad made it. It wasn't quite this gross." He sighed and brooded.

"Suit yourself, I'm eating mine. Did you know that the English say the Romans brought nourishing, thrifty kidney pie to the British shore in ancient times? You're distressing me, not liking my pie. Connie does."

Reginald changed the subject. "There are some nice mantle clocks up in the attic. I'm giving you one." Her frustration over the kidney pie dinner began to fade. She rested her blonde head on her hand, looking at him with her come-hither smile.

"What time do you need to be home?" he asked.

"Not until seven." She giggled and smiled at him. He gobbled up his kidney pie and swallowed it. The bed was not too far away in a small room off the kitchen.

Afterwards, she nuzzled him playfully.

"You're wonderful, the best, Reginald," she murmured in a ten-der, womanly voice.

"Cynthia, Cynthia. It'll always be you. Why didn't you marry me? C'est la vie," Reginald understated, letting it go.

"It's almost six," Cynthia murmured, gaining Reginald's attention. "You know Toby's with Esther and Rebecca. Esther will be good, but she needs to go to bed soon. I need to go."

After arriving home, Cynthia sat comfortably on the sofa holding Esther on her lap. Toby watched television from his recliner. Being close to bedtime, Rebecca played quietly on the floor. Cynthia reached for the open box of raisins on the coffee table in front of her. The phone rang. It rang again. Toby and Cynthia glanced at each other, willing the other person to get up to answer. It rang again. She quickly transferred Esther from her lap to the sofa, leaving the open box of raisins next to her. In the kitchen she picked up the phone.

"Hello?"

"Cynthia! Cynthia!" Toby hollered from the living room. "Quick, help, quick, Cynthia!" The phone dropped from her hand. Panic ran through her like wildfire, putting her blood in motion. She dashed at full speed back to the living room. Esther squirmed on the sofa gagging and choking.

"Oh, my god, she's choking, choking on a raisin! Call an ambulance! Call an ambulance!" Cynthia hysterically screamed.

Time seemed frozen. The ambulance took forever. Toby desperately tried to remember the ABCs of CPR while Cynthia held Esther to coax the raisin out. Nothing they did helped. Finally, the ambulance arrived. The three young emergency medical technicians quickly scooped Esther into the rig.

Toby, stunned, rode in the ambulance with Esther. Cynthia followed them in the family car with Rebecca.

"Mommy? What's the matter, Mommy?" Rebecca's voice sounded loud, like arriving from a faraway place. Cynthia clenched the steering wheel. Only then did she realize that she needed to slow down. "Is Esther hurt, Mommy? Is she hurt? Mommy, is she hurt?"

"Don't yell, Rebecca, sweetheart, please. You don't have to worry because when we get to the hospital you'll see Daddy and Esther." Cynthia managed to speak somewhat calmly, looking at Rebecca's frightened face. Right now, most of all she did not want Rebecca to see her stressful state.

In the ambulance, Toby wanted to grasp Esther's hand, but needed to steady himself on the ambulance's bench for the high-speed ride. He watched his darling little shining star with deepening dread as the boxy truck sped toward the hospital. The EMT assigned to the back of the rig said nothing as he methodically began to intubate the child, hoping to give her air. He pressed the flat blade of the laryngoscope against Esther's tongue. The sight of it made Toby want to vomit. He held his supper down while the technician inserted the endotracheal tube down. Toby made himself stare away out the window. But the utility poles going by looked like a picket fence, making him feel more like vomiting. He secretly hoped the pitching and rolling might help the damned raisin move up or down. The technician slapped a diaper on Esther.

"She's potty trained," Toby protested. He could barely get the words out through his sobs. His shining star was fading away from him.

The ambulance screeched to a stop at the emergency entrance. The team moved the gurney swiftly from the vehicle. They burst through the ER room door bearing little Esther. Her chocolate hair fell in a tangled mess around her unconscious face. The nurse on duty, a graying RN, saw the dull blue color in the beautiful little face. She quickly closed the file she worked on and headed to the cardiac room, knowing her skills would be needed.

Toby, jogging to stay alongside Esther, looked completely unraveled. Fear sculpted his expression and tensed his entire body. His hair hung like a damp mop from running his sweating hands through it.

"She's not breathing," he moaned loudly over and over again. His broken voice mingled with open sobs and echoed through the corridors repeatedly.

"Sir, we need to get information in regard to the child for our records," the young emergency room receptionist said with nonchalant authority, slipping another chart on to the clipboard. She stood to stop him.

"My wife, my wife, is coming behind me." Toby never slowed his pace.

The technician pushed Esther past the ER doors. Toby clung to the side of her cart. A code call came over the intercom, indicating to the ER doctor that a patient presenting acute respiratory distress needed his immediate attention. It took the doctor two and a half minutes to reach the room. An LPN joined the experienced RN in the room.

"What time is it?" the doctor demanded. "What time is it?" he repeated, putting on his gloves.

"Ten forty-one," the RN responded first, making a notation of the time.

"What time do you have for the admittance?"

"The records have not been brought up yet," the LPN said.

No matter what the time, the doctor was right smack up against the deadline for the brain's survival. He assumed permanent damage already occurred.

Meanwhile, Cynthia pulled into the ER parking lot a bit too fast, and the tires kicked up loose asphalt. She put a protective hand across Rebecca as she braked. Then letting out an anxious breath, she ran to the passenger side and retrieved Rebecca. Clutching her hand, they ran toward the ER entrance. The receptionist methodically stood to question Cynthia as she burst through the ER doors. After weeding out which emergency case this woman belonged with, the receptionist busily filled out the forms on her clipboard.

"Yes," stated Cynthia. "I'm her mother."

"Mommy, where is Esther, is she hurt? Where is Daddy?" Rebecca whimpered.

"When am I going to see my little girl and husband?" Cynthia insisted.

"Please take a chair over there, Mrs. Marky." The receptionist motioned to the empty chairs in the ER waiting room. "The doctor is with your daughter at this time."

A clerk rushed briskly into the admissions area entrance.

"They're waiting for the Marky charts. The doc wants them right now," she urged the receptionist. Completing her typing, the receptionist handed the clipboard over to the clerk.

The clerk hurried back to the ER room with the Marky charts on the clipboard.

"Here is the admittance information," the clerk said to the doctor. "Esther Marky, three years old," she stated evenly as she began reading off the chart.

The RN took over the chest compressions from the EMT. Meanwhile, the doctor began his examination.

"What took so long getting those charts here? I need to know the times," the doctor pressed upon the clerk.

"I don't know, sir. Maybe it got dropped into the wrong basket, sir," she answered guardedly then continued to read the chart. The document noted that a team working for a suburban ambulance company brought in the patient. It noted the patient was in obvious trouble when they arrived at the scene. They did an intubation en route. They wrote the drive took three quarters of an hour. The doctor listened while he examined.

"I'm going to make plans for a required course for everyone even remotely involved in this department to know the basics of ER care," the doctor stated to the clerk.

"Yes, sir," she answered.

"The EMTs' job working for the ambulance company should be to transport a patient to the hospital as quickly as possible, beginning with a call-in to the ER department to say they were on their way. They should take a pulse and continue to monitor it up to the time of arrival. The EMT not driving should be applying CPR to the chest. In truth, I suspect the EMTs panicked when they saw the little girl choking," he said angrily.

The doctor, continuing the examination, heard the isolated sounds of captured air. He searched down the throat to scrutinize the intubation.

"Damn it. Damn it," he exclaimed with furious outrage under his breath. The endotracheal tube was in the esophagus. For more than an hour, the oxygen had been bubbling up and down the wrong pipe, never reaching Esther's lungs. Instantly realizing what happened, the graying RN involuntarily lost control of her stoic face and stepped back in disbelief. The moment passed. With swallowed anger, she regained her professionalism.

"Get respiratory in here," the doctor commanded.

The LPN in the room immediately responded, requesting the code. Moments later, the respiratory technician arrived in the room wheeling the portable oxygen tank. Briefed en route about the critical situation, he stood prepared to hold the oxygen mask over the little girl's face. The RN handed the doctor the pediatric laryngoscope. Seconds later, the tube went down the girl's windpipe and reconnected to the portable oxygen tank. The doctor turned on an ophthalmoscope to check the barely constricting pupils of Esther's eyes.

"No signs of returning consciousness." The doctor sighed.

"Not that I can tell." The RN shook her head in agreement. "But look, here is a little more pink where there was blue," she hopefully added. The color confirmed that some oxygen was returning to cells, possibly changing the odds in favor of Esther.

"Monitor this observation further immediately," the doctor ordered the respiratory technician. The doctor and staff had achieved sustaining life in the ER room.

"Make the prep for Children's Hospital and a helicopter at once. I'll speak to the father and the mother, if she's in the waiting room," the doctor said to the RN.

Cynthia sat on the wooden bench in the waiting room staring at the ER entrance doors. Rebecca dozed restlessly while her head lay on Cynthia's lap. When the ER doors opened in the opposite direction than they were accustomed to, Cynthia felt high on exhaustion. The doctor appeared with Toby in tow.

During her uneasy wait, she thought with guilt how jealous she sometimes would be of Esther and Toby. Whatever Esther did, it was okay with Toby. If she wanted the moon, she could have it, if he could reach it for his little star. His pride in how much Esther's features resembled his—her curly chocolate hair, dark eyes, and dimples—sometimes nauseated Cynthia, craving this attention to be lavished on her. The mutual adoration between Esther and Toby definitely showed Esther the center of Toby's world, not Cynthia. Esther chose Toby to undress her and put her to bed, not Mommy. Cynthia hated to acknowledge her jealousy of her little girl and her husband.

Toby collapsed on the bench next to Cynthia. Rebecca twisted and rolled over.

"Will you both come back with me to my office, please?" the doctor spoke quietly.

"Can't we just talk right here?" Toby managed to answer, exhausted.

"No. This is private. Please come with me," the doctor responded.

Toby gathered up a sleepy, wiggling Rebecca into his arms. Obediently they followed the doctor down the hall to his office. Cynthia was bright-eyed as a Barbie doll.

"We will be sending your child in the quickest and smoothest way possible by helicopter to Children's Hospital. She is stabilized and beyond ER care now. This will enable her the best pediatric medical and staff services available of its kind in this area. This will provide her a holding pattern for a severely endangered child. Her little oxygen-starved brain is going to go right on swelling over the next twenty-four hours to forty-eight hours. During that time, there will be hardly anything anyone can do." The doctor paused, giving them direct visual contact.

Toby's eyes reached out to him for more information. His eyes flickered in his face as he silently pleaded for evidence of hope. Cynthia remained impassive.

"They will try to minimize the brain crisis, and that's why your child needs a pediatric facility and staff now," the doctor conveyed with neither optimism nor pessimism.

"Isn't there something else we can do…please?" tearful and helpless Toby begged of the doctor.

"The truth is that the limits of medical expertise that could save this child have just about been reached," the doctor stated, giving no more evidence of hope than he allowed himself to impart. The doctor observed the pitiful love the father showed for his little girl while the mother appeared calmly collected. "All the information in regard to the Children's Hospital will be ready for you at the reception desk on your way out. There may be some other forms to fill out and sign."

The doctor's pager wailed, and he hastily left the room. For Toby and Cynthia, this first and only concrete information about Esther since her admittance to the ER two hours ago left them with confused and exhausted emotions.

Outside on the field, the helicopter landed, later than projected. During the delayed time, little Esther remained in a coma, but stabilized, in the ER facility. So many tubes and bottles attached to her made her body look like separated pieces. The *whisk-a-swish* of the chopper's blades became audible in the beige ER room. The attending older RN took charge of Esther now, since the doctor needed to continue attending other patients. She pressed the code to summon him when notified that the helicopter landed on the ground. Just a few minutes later, two figures in white alongside the doctor hastened into the room. Expertly, they positioned Esther on their gurney to transport her to the helicopter. The helicopter rear door opened, and they rolled Esther inside on her rig. The door closed, and rotors started to turn. The grass flattened against the wind, lifting the air ambulance up.

"Good luck, little Esther," the RN murmured. Looking at the doctor, she softly asked, "A darling little girl. What do you think will happen?"

"I don't think she has much of a chance of making it." He shook his head negatively. "If that child dies, there will almost certainly be enough questions to result in a coroner's autopsy," he confided to the RN. He knew her acute awareness of the faulty intubation during the ambulance ride. Looking away, he saw the Markys walking to the parking lot in a silhouette from the streetlight. He controlled the destiny of their little girl by delivering her onto the best available lifesaving service that he knew of. The Markys, helpless in institutional limbo between this hospital and the next, knew Esther did not belong to them right now. Even her medical history flew with the little star in the aircraft transferring her to the Children's Hospital. "We have to get back to all those patients waiting for us," the doctor directed to the RN, regaining his authority.

Cynthia drove the car back home while Rebecca dozed on the back seat. Toby sat next to her in the front, looking out the window without saying a word. Confused anger crept into his state of mind.

"How are you doing?" she asked him, breaking the silence, her eyes still bright.

"Well, it's not your fault leaving those raisins on the sofa when you went to answer the phone," he reassured her. The idea of being to blame never occurred to Cynthia.

"You don't think so?" Her eyes crinkled up at the corners in surprise at him.

The following morning Toby paced while Cynthia tried to maintain a routine. She made breakfast for Rebecca and helped her get ready for school. Now Rebecca watched for the school bus. Toby, already in contact with the hospital several times, had been informed him that Esther remained in a coma, but stabilized in the ICU. No other information could be given on the telephone. They could only wait. He and his wife could come to the hospital at any time.

"What's taking the damn school bus so long? Don't they know we need to get to the hospital?" he grumbled at Cynthia.

"We're waiting until she's safe on the bus," she told him sternly. "Anyway, they told you there is nothing we can do at the hospital. It's still very early."

For Toby, the wait for the school bus seemed like an eternity. Finally, it rumbled to a stop at their driveway. Cynthia tried to remain calm while walking Rebecca to the bus, holding her hand like any other day. Toby, already in the garage, gunned the car engine.

"God, let's get going!" he shouted, glaring at her.

At the children's hospital, they sat on the wooden bench in the drab gray waiting room.

"How long have we been waiting here? How long has it been? When will they ever come to get us to see her?" Toby sighed in frustration while nudging Cynthia on the arm to get her attention from the book she was reading. Cynthia shrugged her shoulders and returned to her book.

Another thirty minutes passed. Suddenly, a perky young nurse appeared with an apathetic expression on her face.

"Markys?" she questioned. Toby moved his head affirmatively up and down. "Your daughter is still in a coma and on a respirator. Do you want to see her?"

"Of course we want to see her," Toby angrily stammered.

The nurse energetically led them to Esther's room. Tears filled Toby's eyes while he stared silently at the tubes and bottles entangling her body. "After your allotted fifteen minutes, I'll show you to the doctor's office. He wants to meet with you," the nurse said and left the room.

"Oh, Cynthia, what are we going to do?" Toby covered his face with his hands.

Cynthia did not answer. In what seemed like a minute in the silence, not fifteen minutes when the nurse returned to escort them to the office.

"Dr. Williams will be in shortly," she said.

They sat down to wait. Toby fidgeted in his chair, clenching and unclenching his hands. Cynthia calmly opened her book to read again. After twenty minutes, the door swung open. The doctor made a speedy entrance carrying a folder.

After a quick introduction, Dr. Williams said, "I have the file here to review with you from the ER room before the transport here." He read from the medical report. When he finished, he took off his glasses. "Any questions?" An ominous silence crept into the room. After the brief lull, the doctor looked directly at Toby and concluded, "In short, because of the faulty intubation of the endotracheal tube into the esophagus instead of the lungs during the ambulance ride, if she lives, there will be irreversible severe brain damage due to the oxygen deprivation."

Toby covered his face with his hands. Cynthia sat up and fixated her eyes on the doctor.

"Can we please obtain a copy of the report?" she asked without emotion.

"Certainly."

To help time pass, they attempted to eat a late lunch in the hospital cafeteria. The day passed with no change in Esther's condition.

"I'm going to have to leave soon, Toby, to be home for Rebecca when she comes from school," Cynthia gently reminded him, glancing at her watch. "It's two o'clock already. We've only seen Esther three times all day, probably not for a total of thirty minutes." She felt tired and frustrated.

The door to the room opened slowly. A sympathetic-looking older hospital volunteer approached them with a motherly smile.

"Hello, I'm Lorraine. How hard this must be for you. We just all have to put our trust in Jesus's hands, don't we? But I'm here to tell you the request you made, Mr. Marky, to stay the night here in the hospital has been arranged." She lifted the papers from her clipboard.

"What do you think, Cynthia? That's all right with you?"

"Of course, yes, of course. And you'll call me with any changes right away? Okay?" She rummaged in her purse. "Here is all the money and telephone change I have. You need to try to eat some food later." She gave him a goodbye kiss on the cheek.

Driving away, with the armor of distance lengthening between her and the hospital, she whispered, "I must see Reginald. I need to tell him."

PART 2

Dollars and No Sense

CHAPTER 7

Esther vs Et Al.

March 1975

"We're going to be able to bring Esther home tomorrow. She'll require constant care," Cynthia told Connie in a depressed tone on the telephone. "I guess the constant care is going to be me."

"Haven't you looked into an attorney yet to see if you can't at least get some help financially for her care?" Connie asked.

"All of Toby's insurance is through his job. First, that is being examined for coverage. Any investigation for negligence we'll have to initiate on our own. I think we should, especially with the part about the faulty intubation in the records. Toby's looking into personal injury attorneys to take it on as a malpractice. You pay them a percentage of what you win, if the court grants you anything," Cynthia answered. Her hand not holding the telephone twirled the ends of her hair around her fingers one at a time, like her Aunt Natty did.

"I've heard of a law firm that's supposed to be really good with PI. They're even nicknamed German Shepherd, Doberman, and Pit Bull," Connie said. "Let me see what I can find out about them, and their correct names," she added with a laugh.

"Oh thanks, Connie. I'll call you in a couple days. I'd like to have something to help push Toby along," Cynthia said. She sounded brighter.

When Toby came home from work that night, Cynthia approached him with the information from Connie.

"What does she know about attorneys?" he growled. "All I want right now is to leave yesterdays behind us and bring Esther back home, Cynthia."

"Honey, Connie's been living in Port Michigan a long time now. Being a professional photographer, she gets around and knows lots of people in various positions, more than you or me,"

"Okay, okay. First, let's get Esther home."

*****

After only a week passed, Cynthia already began to look worn from the constant care schedule for Esther. Herpes spread over Esther's whole body. She looked crumbly like stale bread. Esther could do nothing for herself. When Cynthia propped her up with pillows, Esther made gurgling noises along with the music Cynthia played on the radio. Toby and Cynthia took turns during the night to check on the connected breathing apparatus for the correct additional oxygen supply. Cynthia had slept through two of her shifts already.

At dinnertime after that first week, Cynthia plopped down on her chair at the kitchen table with Toby and Rebecca. She pushed her plate aside, resting her head on the top of folded hands. She had just finished feeding Esther, washing her, and tucking her in her specialized crib for the night. Toby began Rebecca's dinner first while waiting for Cynthia to come to the table.

"Toby, I have the information from Connie about the law firm," she said.

"Are you feeling okay?" he asked, looking at her surprised. The past week initiated major adjustments for both of them. He did not have the time or energy to notice her. "Gosh, you look terrible," he said. "Are you sure you're okay? You look like you've lost weight, and

94

you're pale. Those circles under your eyes look like layer cakes. Aren't you going to the tanning salon?"

"I'd like to know when? No, I'm not all right. I'm exhausted," she answered. She sighed and slumped down into her chair. "Mr. Sandman just throws dark circles under my eyes instead of bringing sweet dreams after I get up during the night."

Toby studied his wife.

"May I please be excused? I've homework to do," Rebecca said, breaking the uneasy silence.

"Of course you can, darling," Cynthia said. Rebecca left the table, pushing her chair in.

"You've done a good job raising her," Toby said to Cynthia after Rebecca walked out of the kitchen.

"We've done good," she corrected him.

"But we need help now," he said. "Go ahead and contact that law firm Connie is recommending. Get the information we need. Ask Connie to help you make a list of questions. You should probably set up an appointment right away. It'll take some arranging for someone to come in here while we're seeing attorneys and probably going to court. I'll need to take off work too. Taking off work will be the easy part."

March 1976

In court, a year later, the defense attorney roughly questioned the nurse on the witness stand.

"Yes, the endotracheal tube was in the esophagus," the ER nurse from the night shift of Esther's admittance testified without hesitation.

"Faulty intubation occurred during the ambulance ride. The attending doctor informed me that if the child would die," she continued, "there would be enough questions to result in a coroner's autopsy."

Murmurs rose in the courtroom. The judge nodded toward the defense attorney.

"The defense rests."

Until the testimony from the nurse, the proceeding of the lawsuit had not progressed in Esther's favor. They waited six hours for the decision from the jury. Finally, it came. The amount that the Markys asked for in Esther's malpractice suit was five million dollars. The jury granted Esther Marky three million dollars in settlement for her future care and financial requirements. The law firm's percentage amounted to 30 percent, leaving Esther two million one hundred thousand dollars. Toby and Cynthia were appointed joint guardians of Esther's new wealth.

First, they built a house for Esther under a canopy of old, shady maple trees located atop a hill in a new developing suburb. The Markys added an adjoining in-ground, handicap-equipped swimming pool constructed for her rehabilitation. The house's great room combined with the kitchen. New chairs in this area had wheels so Cynthia could easily move about while holding Esther. The attached three-car garage opened to a handicap entrance to the great room. Through the center of the house a long, wide hallway led to the master bedroom at the end. The master bedroom's adjacent huge twelve-by sixteen-foot bathroom, complete with spa, shone with matching state-of-the-art Kohler fixtures for Esther. One of the other two bathroom doors went to the azure pool for Esther and the other to her bedroom. The other door from Esther's bedroom opened to the hall. Three more bedrooms opened to the hall, one being Rebecca's with its own bath. The other two rooms shared a full bath between them with red Kohler fixtures for Esther's care too. A caregiver came in for her daily now.

Before the long hallway, a formal dining room pleasantly presented itself. A greenish marble-top sideboard stretched along one wall. It came from Aunt Natty, and before that from the glorious days of the decorated Golden Bounty mansion. Inside the front entrance, a parlor-style living room welcomed guests. These rooms were also for Esther's care and handicap requirements.

Toby and Cynthia took turns monitoring Esther during the night every other night. Cynthia awoke late this Tuesday morning. *Goodness,* she thought. *I must have slept through my check on Esther.*

Quickly, she pulled on a pink silk robe and saw Toby off for work. He continued to work at the department store. Rebecca, dressed in a pretty purple floral matching skirt and blouse, waited at the doorway for the school bus. The bus came. She boarded it for school. Cynthia made plans to shop that day after the care provider arrived. She walked down the hall to Esther's room to bathe and dress her. In the unusually quiet room, her brain did not realize the absence of the usual gurgling breathing noises.

Cynthia bent over to pick her up. Esther felt cold. She began to rock her to wake her up. Then she opened her hands, letting the body drop back into the crib in a stiff lump. The silence in the room engulfed her. She stepped back, rigidly upright. Her mouth hung on open.

"Esther's dead," Cynthia gasped out the words. "Oh my god! She's dead." She clenched her fists. Her polished fingernails dug into the palms of her hands. Then she gripped the side of the crib with her frame shaking. "Esther's dead." She stared at the motionless, stiff body. A hint of blue surrounded Esther's lips. "She must have suffocated during her sleep. Oh, no, no, no, no." She tossed back her head, moaning. "Oh, my god. I slept through my shift last night." She started to sob. Then a split second later, she regained her staunch composure. "No, no, of course it's not my fault," Cynthia assured herself, winding a strand of hair around her finger.

She backed away from the crib. Turning toward the door she exited the room. Walking down the hall with slow, deliberate steps, she rubbed the fingers of her left hand against the fingers on the other hand to help her think. *I must call Toby immediately to tell him and get him home,* she thought. *He can handle this nightmare by himself. He won't want me involved with funeral arrangements for his precious Esther anyway.* "Gosh," she said, pausing before picking up the phone to dial. "I'll need to shop to buy new black clothes to wear. Surely Hardy will come."

June 1976, A Year After Esther's Death
Cynthia and Toby

"All right, all right, I'll go, I'll go," Toby relented.

"It would be nice if you would," Cynthia said, sweetly smiling at him.

He had just finished listening to his wife make more plans with Connie on the phone about the Parkton cousins' reunion that she planned for this coming August at The Lodge.

"We'll rent our own place this time," Toby ranted. "We can afford to rent wherever we want now. Nobody is staying with us. That includes your bloody first cousin, Hardy. We'll see plenty of him buzzing around you all the time anyway. Buzz…he sure is something. Why doesn't he get those stained teeth fixed? He has plenty of money. And that Reginald, he's another one tripping over his dong to look at you."

"Toby, please stop the language," she interjected. She tried to control how irritated he made her.

"When we're at The Lake, you spend more time with those two freaks than me. That Reginald, what does he do anyway? Tend bar at The Lodge, screw around with some old boats with Billy, and booze it up with your Aunt Natty. That whole damn lake is incestuous, just plain incestuous. Now you have Connie involved. Lucky her. She's not even a relative. That place isn't just incestuous, it's inbred. Billy Benwolfski is the only square shooter up there. Sometimes I wonder if he's all there too. At least a person can get a straight answer and conversation out of him. Yeah, it sure is something at that lake of yours," he said, scuffling his feet across the floor to move the kitchen chair with wheels on the bottom to the refrigerator for another beer. He crossed his arms defiantly across his chest.

Cynthia let it all go past her. She had heard it before.

"Grab that bottle of Chardonnay or that bottle of Pinot Grigio while you're there," she said, not paying any attention to his ranting. What ensembles she would wear at the reunion entered her mind. She needed to start shopping now. She thought to herself, *It'll be in August, three months away, and at the time Hardy always comes. It'll be nice and warm.* "Hardy doesn't have any intention of staying with us, Toby. He'll rent his own cottage like usual. Then maybe stay at Connie's," she spoke absentmindedly. "We'll probably have our combined August birthday party that week, too, for Rebecca, Amber, and Mitchell's two boys. All the little second cousins together on Connie's pontoon boat. Won't it be wonderful? Isn't it nice that Mitchell's coming with his family? Natty's offered for them to stay in her apartment with her. It's been years since he's come out to the Lake in the summer," she said to Toby while pouring a glass of Chardonnay.

"That's because he's smart," Toby snapped at her. "And that Connie, she thinks that because she's a professional photographer and teacher that she's some kind of women's libber. Well, good on her. And isn't it the cat's ass that she supposedly comes from some money too," Toby sarcastically added.

"She's going to take pictures at the reunion dinner at The Lodge. She isn't charging any money," Cynthia stated in defense of her friend. "Your negative attitude about The Lake slides downhill daily. Just chuck it," Cynthia said, raising her voice back at him.

August 1976, Reunion

Cynthia saw summer pass to August without her frequent visits to The Lake. Every other Monday she arranged to meet Reginald on his day off from The Lodge at Connie's home in Port Michigan.

The Parkton cousins' family reunion week finally arrived. The Parkton cousins, Hardy, his brother Mitchell, and their families flew from Connecticut. Toby, Cynthia, and Rebecca drove to the Lake in their two-year-old DMC custom van, which they had bought for Esther. The cottage they rented, built directly on the bank of the water, was located on the same road as The Lodge. It faced west to the spectacular views of the sunsets from the splendid shore. The two bedrooms and two bathrooms were furnished in country cottage decor, with lots of dusty blue. A hand-carved sign hung over the entrance that read "Cottage Sweet Cottage."

Reginald observed the night of the reunion dinner in The Lodge from behind the bar. He attended to the Parkton cousins' drink needs. Aunt Natty was, of course, included too. Connie took pictures of various assembled groups in front of the fireplace with the keystone that read "Where friends meet hearts warm."

"How funny." Reginald chuckled, nodding toward Connie taking another group picture as he mixed a JB and water for Hardy.

"It's great, great." Hardy grinned, lighting a cigarette. "Connie, take one of all four second cousins together now," Hardy said, bouncing over to her from his barstool with cigarette and drink in his hand. "And then take one of Great-Aunt Natty with the four little ones."

"Sure thing," Connie said. "Round them up."

"Cynthia looks like a million," Hardy said to Reginald after returning to the bar. She wore a long smocked shoulder-less dress. The print was a red-orange floral on a soft golden yellow all-cotton background. The rich chocolate of her tan provided a luxuriant backdrop for it. To ensure the Midas touch, she wore a five-strand gold necklace wrapped loosely about her graceful neck. It dipped into her bosom, draping and shimmering.

"That's because she has a million." Reginald chuckled, nervously running his hand over his nose and mouth. Cynthia swished her way to the bar, stopping to chat as she progressed.

"Another champagne, please," she told Reginald.

"Here, take my chair." Hardy quickly stood up as he offered. He motioned to his barstool, holding his cocktail. "You look like a princess tonight." He pushed up his glasses, swooning over her. He raised himself up and down on the balls of his feet, sighing, content just to be in her aura.

"That lady over there is trying to get your attention," Reginald said to Hardy, pointing to the piano bar.

"Be right back," Hardy said, looking toward the blonde woman.

"I can get away from everyone and come to your house after this is over," Cynthia whispered to Reginald.

Cynthia and Reginald exchanged sultry eye contact. She said nothing more, sipping her champagne. Reginald lighted a cigarette and continued to fill drink orders. After his father passed two years ago, Reginald's mother continued to live in the family home three houses down from The Lodge. Reginald moved back in to take care of her.

As the dinner part of the reunion wound down at The Lodge, the cousins made plans to meet at Noble's.

"Coming over to Noble's, Reginald?" Hardy asked.

"Don't know yet, my mother needs to go the bathroom about eleven o'clock."

"I'm riding over to Noble's with Connie," Cynthia told Toby. "I can tell you're already sick of this and don't want to come. I'll get a ride back to the cottage."

"Oh, I'm sure you will manage that," he shot back at her.

Toby drove the short distance to the rental cottage. After drinking a beer, he decided to go to Noble's instead of sitting alone. Rebecca stayed with the group of younger cousins at Amber's grandfather's house. The quietness of the cottage disturbed him. With Billy tending bar at Noble's, he could probably stand going there. Toby steered the van to drive along the lake road over to Noble's. Arriving ten minutes later, he walked into the crowded cocktail lounge. Billy spotted him from behind the bar. Toby looked around. He saw Connie, but no Cynthia.

"Did Cynthia come over here with someone, Billy? Gimme a beer," Toby said.

"Nope, haven't seen her yet," Billy said while hustling to serve drink orders.

"Everyone is here, but no Cynthia," Toby said. His irritation started to show. He rubbed the back of his neck as he pushed his way through the full bar packed with people from the reunion to where Hardy leaned on the bar. He figured if anyone knew Cynthia's whereabouts Hardy would. He always watched her from behind those ugly horn-rimmed glasses.

"Hey, Hardy, did Cynthia come over with you?"

"Nope, thought she'd come with you because she's not here, yet."

"Well, shit," Toby sputtered. "She's left behind at The Lodge. It's a mix-up. I'll go pick her up."

Toby raced back to The Lodge on the double. After jumping out of the van, he bolted up the entrance stairs to find the doors locked tight for the night. The Lodge, dark and still, did not even have Reginald cleaning up. Then the shock of the puzzle hit him. No Reginald cleaning up and no Cynthia at Noble's.

"Jesus Christ," he exclaimed furiously. He sped past the three houses literally winging his way to Reginald's driveway. Swiftly, but quietly, he began walking down it. Then as he drew closer to the house, he distinctively heard the pleasurable sound of lovemaking floating from Reginald's open windows on the summer night's breeze. He stood still, frozen like a cement statue. Then enraged, he raced to the locked kitchen door. He raised up his arm and smashed the glass with a fierce blow from his fist. Reaching inside, he snapped back the lock.

Hearing the sound of glass breaking, "What's that noise?" Cynthia whispered between breaths.

"Don't know, wind…" Reginald panted.

Outside Toby suddenly stopped short. His manner shifted. He drew back his hand, tucking it into his pocket. Turning around, he calmly walked back down the driveway. The floating sounds of lovemaking hushed. He slid into his van, shutting the door with barely a stir of sound. Boiling inside with indignation, he fumed as he forced himself to drive back down the road to the rental cottage. Once inside he mixed himself a drink and paced, unraveling the discovery.

"Cynthia and Reginald. Stupid me. Should have seen the damned thing long, long ago. Damn it, damn it, damn it," he bitterly swore. "I'm a real laughingstock. Well, April fool on me," he said. Shaking his head, he slammed the drink down on the table.

Twenty minutes later, Cynthia and Reginald's shoes crunched the broken glass inside Reginald's house on their way out. The noise echoed in the murky darkness.

"See, the wind did rattle the door and break the glass," Reginald whispered, reaching to unlock it. "Jeez, it's unlocked," Reginald exclaimed under his breath.

"It couldn't have been the wind. I know we locked the door." Cynthia's muffled voice sounded alarmed.

"Yeah," Reginald agreed with harbored consternation.

They both knew. Apprehensive, Cynthia briskly moved herself along on the road back to the rental cottage. Now the enticing summer escape was snuffed out by the murkiness of the night. The Milky Way and August moon did not twinkle on the Lake. Cynthia's hand hesitated timidly on the handle of the cottage door. Fearful of making any noise to wake Toby, she silently undressed and slid into bed next to him.

"Have a good time, Cynthia?"

Cynthia started. "You're still awake. Yeah, it's so nice to see everyone. I wish you'd come over too," she tensely managed. She lay rigidly on her side with her back toward him, not moving.

"Who brought you back here?" he roughly asked.

"Ah…Connie," she said.

"Funny, I didn't hear her car."

Before falling into an uneasy sleep, she thought, *We both knew Toby broke the window when we were by the door at Reginald's house. Toby knows. I must see Reginald. I need to tell him.*

CHAPTER 8

Road Trip

September 1976, Pregnant

Cynthia dreamily pondered how magical it would be to have Reginald's baby. She checked her calendar for the dates surrounding the summer night at his mother's house. Ten, seven, eleven, she counted out the days on her calendar. *There isn't a possibility of anyone else,* she ecstatically mused. When she knew for a fact, secretly she planned to drive up to The Lake to tell Reginald the fantastic news.

"Reginald, I can get away Thursday to come to The Lake. I'll meet you at Natty's around eleven," Cynthia told him on the telephone.

"I can hardly wait," he said with exhilaration.

"You remember where we hid the key, right?" she asked.

"Yeah, yeah, of course."

Thursday, Reginald sat at Natty's round oak table smoking a cigarette early, waiting. Just minutes later, though it seemed like an hour, Cynthia walked in. It didn't take them long to change their location to the four-poster bed. After the luscious encounter, they returned to the table.

"I've forgotten how gorgeous the fall light is coming through the windows," Cynthia said.

The light refracted by a natural filter of trees with gold leaves waving at the sky made the lake look misty.

"Guess what, Reginald," she began, watching him. "Well, I'm pregnant from the night in August at your mother's house, and I'm going to have your baby."

"Oh yeah?" He lighted a cigarette, looking straight at her, shocked at the news. "How do you know it's mine?" he asked, on the defense.

"It is for sure. I counted the days out on the calendar."

"So I'm going to be a father," he said, trying to digest the idea. "Well, now you're going to have to divorce that Toby guy and marry me. His only kid is dead. She was the object of his affection in his life, not you," Reginald retorted.

Cynthia represented all that Reginald knew of a love dearer than life itself. His hands trembled taking a drag off cigarette, thinking. Then his face took on a ghastly pallor.

"When I get older, I get more stupid," he said. "Oh, foolish me to think you'd marry me when all the money is yours and Marky's together now. What a joke." His whole soul hungered and thirsted for her. By night and day he dreamed of her. It would be always be Cynthia, the love of his life.

October 1976, Florida

Billy called Toby, telling him on the phone, "Here's the deal. We can leave really early. We'll take turns driving. Two days, we'll be in Florida. Plus, it would be cheap. Hey, it would be great, just like when we went before in college."

"Cheap," Toby repeated. He didn't care about cheap anymore, but his interest in the adventure with Billy already ignited him. "Hmm, when are you thinking about? Well anyway, Cynthia and I are trying to work things out and get back together, you know. So it'll be the two of us. She'll go as soon as I tell her about it. You know how she eats up baking in the sun. Sometimes I think the sun could burn a path right through her skin. But it's all she needs besides me," he said and laughed smugly.

"You guys are trying to get back together." Billy chuckled too. "Would be shits and grins to have Cynthia along for the ride. No slack with her around. Never know what the hell to expect. Sure. What about your job?"

Toby kept his department store job despite inheriting Esther's estate. "I can take off. I'm promoted to a manager position now. Remember? Just requires some arranging. What did you do? Quit Noble's?"

"No, they're closing for ten days to do some repairs and toning up before the holiday season starts. You know, the Christmas parties and all that BS."

"When?" Toby wanted the exact dates.

"Starting the second week in October. It's still nice and warm in Florida then. Hurricane season should be over, right, Toby?" Billy answered.

"Maybe that'll be the week her cousin comes to celebrate his birthday. Definitely count on us going then. To miss seeing him would be all right. Doesn't matter, I don't see him anyway. You know she comes up to the Lake for that alone," Toby grumbled.

"Yeah, Hardy never used to do the birthday thing. Now he does. Strange guy. Must not have any friends at home. Well, call me. I'm paying for this call." Billy said goodbye and hung up.

When Toby told Cynthia that Billy called with his idea of going to Florida, she agreed immediately.

"But, honey, when you call him back, tell him that we'll take our DMC van. It is so roomy and comfortable." She began thinking of what she would buy to wear. Being pregnant with Reginald's baby from the tryst in August, this would be her last chance not to wear maternity clothes for the next seven months.

Two weeks passed quickly from when Billy first called. Cynthia shopped daily at Helen of Troy, buying more clothes. Toby would try to take time to lunch with her. "I can't believe that none of last summer's clothes are available anymore. Not even on the sale racks," she complained to him.

Toby made arrangements with his mother to stay with Rebecca before beginning the road trip with Billy. The first morning Billy pulled over so Cynthia could throw up. The next morning Billy pulled over so Cynthia could throw up again.

"Say, what's the deal?" Billy directed at Toby.

"She's pregnant with *her* baby," Toby sharply answered.

Billy eyed his friend, thinking, *Her baby, what a strange way to put it.* He pondered it some.

They drove straight through to Fort Lauderdale. There her morning sickness subsided. Beginning in Fort Lauderdale, she insisted on suntanning on the beach. After all, it was fall now. The days would be short up in Wisconsin. She could still wear a two-piece swimming suit nicely. At Fort Lauderdale she donned a baby blue two-piece. The blue matched her eyes. A sheer open-weave poncho pretended to be a cover-up. The color, a touch more toward aqua than baby blue, completed the ensemble. Toby and Billy found a beach club where they could watch sports and have a couple of beers. Cynthia absolutely insisted on stopping at all the beaches on the way north. At each beach she lounged on a chaise with her pocketbook of the day, adorned in a new swimming suit ensemble. After Fort Lauderdale, they motored north to West Palm Beach, then Vero Beach, then Cocoa Beach, then Daytona Beach, and finally Saint Augustine Beach. Toby and Cynthia fought most of the time. Billy thought the only thing interesting was the way the beaches changed going north. The beaches became steeper and more gravelly as Cynthia's suntan became deeper and more golden.

When Billy's vacation neared the last days, he was finished too. At the last and most northern beach in Florida, Saint Augustine Beach, he flatly stated to Toby, "We're driving straight through now till we're home."

After the return, Cynthia continued trying to work out the marriage with Toby for the sake of her daughter, Rebecca, and her and Reginald's child to come. During the winter, Cynthia and Reginald continued meeting at Connie's house in Port Michigan.

Spring 1977, Samuel Marky

In May, Cynthia gave birth to Samuel Marky. Cynthia and Reginald decided on the name Samuel if the new baby came into the world a boy. Cynthia again insisted on a religious name. Reginald said "C'est la vie" to the name picking. At least Samuel seemed more civilized than Elijah, in his opinion. Samuel, being designated with the last name Marky, didn't impress Reginald or his mother either. Between children and money issues, Cynthia and Toby's marriage constantly remained pressured. It continued to deteriorate. Toby, being appointed the trustee to manage the estate, handled the finances. Cynthia did not realize that monies were transferred out of the estate as the marriage snowballed toward an impending divorce.

"But I thought there was a college fund set aside for Rebecca," Cynthia insisted to her attorney.

"All the financial reports submitted to me from Mr. Marky's attorney indicated there was not. They appear conclusive and in order," he answered while shuffling papers on his oversized desk. "I think splitting the remaining portion of the estate exactly half and half as Mr. Marky's attorney is agreeing to would be prudent for you to consider seriously at this time. Roughly $900,000 apiece, including splitting the real estate assets."

August 1977, Hardy's Annual Visit

Connie drove her pontoon boat over to The Lodge to suntan with Cynthia on the dock. Cynthia got up to grab a line to help tie the boat. The newly purchased Tacori platinum and diamond ring on Cynthia's right hand glistened in the sunlight. She wore a pink two-piece bathing suit with a studded dynamo outline of each breast. A matching pink beach bag lay in a heap on the dock. She flung a sheer French, pink silk poncho cover-up near the bag. On her recent shopping extravaganza to Michigan Avenue's Magnificent Mile in Chicago, she also acquired the gold horn hoop earrings from Peacock's that shone as she bent over to tie the line.

"Hi, Cynthia, what's happening? How are you doing? What a fabulous bathing suit," Connie complimented. Then she pointed. "Look at that, it's Reginald with Billy on *Temperance*." Cynthia, who had already returned to her prone position on the dock, now leaned on one elbow eyeing the approaching boat. Reginald maneuvered a perfect landing, of course.

"Come with us. I'm meeting up with Hardy and that strange guy with him, whatever his name is, over at Noble's. Oh yeah, and Billy's going to work," Reginald called to Cynthia from his boat.

"I can't." Cynthia raised herself up onto her arm to talk to him. "Aunt Natty is watching Rebecca while Baby Samuel is napping up in her apartment."

"What do you have to stay here for then?" Reginald badgered.

Cynthia did not answer.

"I'll go," Connie interjected. "You don't mind, do you, Cynthia? I know I just got here, but I need to give Billy some crap about his upcoming betrothal. Right, Billy?" Connie raised her voice to be sure he could hear her over the gurgling Chris Craft.

"No, no, go. Leave your boat here. Tell everyone to come here with you on your way back. I'll have Rebecca and the baby down here at the dock by then. Aunt Natty too," Cynthia said.

"Come on. We've got to get going. I need to check in at two o'clock!" Billy yelled to Connie.

"Great, thanks. See you later, Cynthia. And you get to see your son then, Reginald," Connie threw out at him, climbing into the boat.

Noble's was jammed as usual on a Sunday. People played bocce ball on the front lawn nearest the Lake. Elegant fiberglass boats and glistening mahogany boats lined the pier.

"Look at all the money floating there." Connie shook her head.

Spotting a barely large enough space on a pier, Reginald zipped into it perfectly. Billy leaped onto the pier to tie up. "See ya. I've got to hurry." He hustled up the pier to the restaurant. Reginald and Connie walked down the pier, crossed the outdoor deck, and entered the lounge area. They spotted Hardy and the gentleman with him at Billy's end of the bar. They waved to Hardy that they were heading his way. It appeared Hardy must have just arrived at the bar as he did not have a drink yet. This was the first time they would all be getting together since Hardy's arrival Friday. He had rented a cottage for himself and the man with him for the week. He stashed his daughter, Amber, safely with her grandparents.

After hellos and a quick hug with Connie, Hardy introduced the man with him.

"Reginald, meet my friend, Carel Van Kampen." Hardy introduced Carel. Reginald and Van Kampen shook hands. Then turning to Connie, he said, "And this lady is Connie Fillmore. She's my friend I told you about. I crash at her pad sometimes. Connie, this is Carel." Connie shook hands with Carel.

"Nice to meet you. I can't help noting a little accent. Do you mind if I ask you where you are from?" Connie questioned.

"Amsterdam," Van Kampen replied.

"He's helping me with some business while he's in the United States. I thought I'd bring him along to see the Lake and play." Hardy tacked on this brief explanation in regard to his friend Van Kampen, pushing up his horn-rimmed glasses.

"Oh." Connie glanced at him, quickly taking him in. Carel Van Kampen stood six foot three, had a slender waist, and broad shoulders. Well dressed, he wore a blue Brooks Brothers shirt with a polka-dotted yellow ascot and gray trousers. His brown leather belt matched his Netherlands Van Bommel leather loafers. The belt boasted an opulent gold buckle bearing his initials, CVK, in diamonds. His weathered face had a hard edge to it. The bags under his eyes reminded Connie of the cartoon character Droopy Dog. At the time, Connie didn't think further about him. After all, Hardy was the president of the First National Bank of Connecticut, and probably associated with all sorts of characters.

"Hey, you guys. How about some drinks to whet your whistles?" Billy cheerfully motioned at them, comfortably working behind the bar already.

"I'll buy, in honor of Reginald's new baby. Billy already told us the Florida story." Hardy laughed, still amused from just having heard it the first thing from Billy, even before a drink.

"Hell, the best part is when Toby said 'Cynthia is having *her* baby.' But it only took me a second or two to figure it out," Billy smartly said.

"If Hardy's buying, I'll have Myers and diet," Reginald blurted out.

"Rest of you, the usual?" Billy began making the drinks. "Carel, what about you?"

"What do you have for beer?"

"Just for you, I have Amstel," Billy said obligingly. He had heard "Amsterdam."

"Okay, that is good. I will take it."

"Coming back with us to Natty's?" Connie asked Hardy. "We'll get tagalongs from Billy for the boat ride. Cynthia said we should ask you to stop back with us, plus my pontoon boat's there. She's sunbathing on the pier."

"Something new in that? Sure we'll come. I haven't seen Natty yet either," Hardy said. He grinned in excitement, showing his nasty tobacco-stained teeth. "Let's drink up here and get some tagalongs. I'm anxious to be out on the lake and to see Cynthia." He turned to Carel. "My cousin Cynthia is a bronzed goddess from the *Iliad*. Wait until you see her," he said, beaming at Carel.

Carel agreed wholeheartedly when he saw Cynthia on The Lodge dock. Connie hopped off *Temperance* to tie up. Then the rest stepped up and off. Hardy introduced Cynthia and Carel. They exchanged interested glances during the introduction. Hardy and Cynthia exchanged a hello kiss on the mouth. Reginald observed it all, catching Cynthia's eyes in direct contact for an instant. Natty sashayed down the dock with a cigarette dangling from her lilac lips. Rebecca and Susan Sunshine followed her. Natty held Baby Samuel in her arms. Rebecca, seven years old now, pranced along in the image of her mother with vanilla curls. She wore a robin egg blue sundress with two matching ribbons in her hair. Susan Sunshine, Natty 's replacement dog for the deceased Sunbonnet Sue, wore a darling day-glow green and pink flowered Lilly ribbon around her neck. They made a ludicrous visual parade in the afternoon sun.

When Reginald, Connie, and Billy had left for Noble's, Cynthia changed her swimsuit ensemble, anticipating Hardy would be with them when they returned. Now for their arrival back, she donned a coppery two-piece swimsuit trimmed with a diffusion of gold. Very close in color to her tanned body, the initial illusion transformed her into appearing almost naked except for the outline of gold.

"You look good, Hardy. Here, Reginald, take your baby so I can give Hardy a hug." Natty gave her nephew a warm welcome hug. "I'm so glad, Reginald, your dear mother insisted on changing his name from Marky to Haley as it should be. You know from the time of his birth until the legal switch, she was distressed that, he, Samuel, her only grandchild, did not carry the Haley name," Natty said to Reginald.

"Natty, I'm going to interrupt to introduce you to my friend visiting from Amsterdam. Natty, this is Carel Van Kampen." Hardy introduced Carel. "Heard about your divorce Natty, we'll talk later," he added.

"Amsterdam? You must have flown out of Schiphol. My former husband and I would use Schiphol sometimes, but usually we would use Lelystad with our Lear. We would go to the Miljonairs Beurs," Natty chatted on.

"Yes," he answered somewhat on the alert. "I am very pleased to make your acquaintance, Miss Natty." Carol tried not to show surprise at the Amsterdam information Natty immediately imparted, showing someone here was that familiar with it.

"Well, come up to the apartment for drinks," Natty invited the group.

"Great, my tagalong is gone." Hardy turned his plastic cup upside down, making his point clear.

The group climbed up the grassy slope from the lake to Natty's apartment. Reginald carried his little baby, Samuel. They gathered on the comfortable white wicker furniture in the screened porch. A cooling light southwest breeze blew through the porch.

"It's self-serve here," Natty reminded everyone. "Carel, you need to help yourself too. The bar is always set up on the Hoosier to the left of the sink. Tell me, Hardy, where are you renting this year?"

"By the marina for a week, close to everything. Can almost walk everywhere, except maybe Noble's. Say, can we use your phone?"

"Sure, you remember where it is," Natty briefly contemplated Carel as the two men left the porch.

Momentarily, Hardy returned to the porch with his JB and water, leaving Van Kampen on the phone.

"Perhaps I'll plan a cocktail party while you're here, Hardy," Natty suggested as Hardy planted himself next to Cynthia on the white wicker sofa.

"Too early to make commitments, Natty. Let's play it by ear," Hardy shook his head.

"Tell me more about your bronzed cousin from the *Iliad*," Carel questioned Hardy later back at their rental cottage. Carel became even more intrigued when he heard the part about Cynthia's upcoming divorce. Hardy, enormously pleased with himself for mustering Carel's interest in Cynthia right from the get-go, gladly embellished her situation to him. Hardy's mind fantasized about having Cynthia respectfully married to Carel in Connecticut, ever so close to him.

CHAPTER 9

El Pleamar

January 1980, Port Michigan

"Of course you can come, Connie," Cynthia coaxed. "It's a whole month away. Like I said, it's the last chance I'll have to use the time-share. Toby's getting it in the divorce. You know it's paradise at El Pleamar. You'll love it. We bought right on the first floor overlooking the Pacific for Esther. We've only used it the one time. The view just takes your breath away."

"I'm sure I'd love it. I've never been to Mexico. That's not the problem. The problem is to see if I can arrange to alter my work schedule with my boss. Probably I can. February starts to slow down. For just one week I think it'll be feasible," Connie answered, already thinking about scuba diving. "And what an opportunity to speak Spanish." She weighed the two good reasons to go against work rescheduling.

"Yeah, it would be a great chance for you to practice your Spanish," Cynthia continued to urge. "Guess what. Hardy will be able to get away for one week too. He'll meet us. Won't it be fun? You know when Toby and I vacationed there the one time with the kids and Billy, you were dying to come with us." Cynthia assumed Connie would go because she always believed Connie was jealous of her and wanted to do everything she did.

"Yeah, I would have loved to come. But I just couldn't take off work. Maybe this time," Connie answered, tilting her head to the side, not surprised at Cynthia's comment about dying to go with them. Her lips drew a thin line. She let it go.

February 1980, El Pleamar

After more than a year, the Marky divorce would finally be settled in March. In the property disbursement, the full six weeks of the time-share in El Pleamar became Toby's. At the time of purchase, Toby pushed hard for the time-share. The concept of joint property ownership had just started. He thought it a tremendous investment. Cynthia's property portion of the divorce settlement gave her the excessive house they built for Esther's needs when she was alive. At this point, Cynthia planned to continue to live there with her two children. Rebecca, now a pretty and popular girl, attended fifth grade. She received excellent marks in her studies. As joint heirs to Esther's estate, Cynthia and Toby evenly split the remaining assets between them. It surprised Cynthia how monies dwindled in the short time since Esther's death. The fact that Rebecca's college fund disappeared bothered her considerably.

"I adopted Rebecca when I married Cynthia," Toby said. "I think of her as my daughter and fully agree to pay child support for her as the court decides," Toby told his attorney. "As for her college fund, it's not my duty to replace it, like Cynthia wants. What's gone is gone. Joint custody of Rebecca is totally acceptable with me too. However, Samuel is not, in any part, my responsibility."

*****

Connie did arrange her work schedule to take the third week in February off. The Wednesday before Cynthia and Connie planned to leave, Cynthia drove Samuel to the Lake for his father to take care of him while she played at El Pleamar. She anticipated a bedroom romp, letting her hair fall about her shoulders. Plus, she intended to have her hair all cut off anyway the following morning.

After arriving at Reginald's house, she put Samuel to nap while she and Reginald renewed their love-filled relationship in his bed.

"Since your mother is passed now, I don't understand why you don't have any money," Cynthia said, toying with his hair after the sexual encounter. "Why didn't your parents have any money left, your father being an attorney? How could they have spent everything plus mortgage the house?" Cynthia broke away from him, moping about his not receiving an inheritance. "I thought for sure you'd inherit some money."

"Nope. Dad spent some time in his office, and a lot of time at his other 'office' meeting his cohorts every day for martini lunches, you know. Then he'd go back to his office for a nap. That didn't bring money in. The house is being sold. I don't have money to make any mortgage payment."

"Will you get any money after the house is sold?" she pressed on.

"Probably not. It looks like it'll be even-Steven when all the bills are paid off and the probate attorney is paid."

"But where will you live?"

"Maybe at Natty's for a while. She doesn't have any money either. So she says. I could help her out with some repairs she wants and pay a little rent for her second bedroom. I don't know yet. The house isn't sold anyway. I've a roof over my head still," he said in a joking way, trying to change the subject.

"But," she continued, "how could you stand the stink at Natty's with those six cats and dog? She doesn't clean anything, drinks that cheap wine by the gallon. She's insane when it comes to her animals. That ammonia smell in her house from cat urine makes me stagger. I won't go there when I come to the Lake. She doesn't keep herself up at all anymore. At least when she was married to moneybags, she always dressed distinctively and looked fantastic, even though she mostly dressed in Lilly's from her little boutique in South Beach. She kept her hair dyed all the time then too. Now all the roots are black and gray. I told her I'm pretty disgusted with her, and that she needed to get rid of those cats. She just looked at me, poured herself a glass of wine, and twirled her dirty hair around her finger. Then she said she named one of the cats, the one with six toes after you, Reginald. You two could cocktail together though, couldn't you?" The accusation hung in the air.

"Well, I don't have a problem with Natty. I can't help it that she spent all of her divorce settlement and her alimony is running out. Who cares anyway. Maybe yes, maybe no. She can drink cheap wine for all I care. She claims it's all she can afford. Who knows. I don't know and I don't care. And I don't mind helping her out with small chores at all. She's kind and always as generous as she can be. She's talking about taking the ex, old moneybags, back to court in Alaska for more money. I'm not sleeping outside." He nervously ran his hand over his nose. "Cynthia, why don't you marry me after your divorce is over? I'd move to Port Michigan and get a real job. You know the Blackings at the Lake always offer me work at their cement company in the city. I'd take them up on their offer. Marry me, Cynthia."

"No, Reginald. Your attitude about work wouldn't change. It'd be the same there as it is here. I'm getting the house in the divorce, but assets have dwindled drastically." She frowned, staring up at the ceiling. "I must have security. Rebecca is popular now and needs clothes too. Plus Samuel, your shamefully low ninety dollars a month child support—that I don't always get—doesn't begin to cover his needs. No, Reginald, no," she said with the distinct emphasis on not always receiving his measly small payment hanging in the air. She propped herself up on one elbow, initiating an armor of distance from him.

"I can't give you more money than I have, Cynthia. I'm saying I'll get a real job if you'll marry me. You're the love of my life and the mother of my child." He looked at her, imploring her honestly, yet distressed by his rabid longing for her. Silence loomed in the room. Then Samuel began to wake up. "Why don't you ask Hardy for money? I'm sure he'd give it to you in a heartbeat. He's got plenty. You're meeting him in Mexico, right?" Reginald sarcastically showed his jealousy. He sat up on the bed to reach for a cigarette from the nightstand.

"Well, I asked you to go, but as usual you didn't have any money. I can't pay for you. I need to get going. It's two hours back home, and I must be there when Rebecca comes from school," she said. Irritated with him, she started to pull on her pink lace underpants. "Get dressed. I need to show you what I packed for Samuel."

*****

A week later Cynthia picked up Connie at her house at three in the morning. Cynthia purchased a Hilton Hotel travel package for O'Hare, allowing her to leave her car parked there for their week of vacation. It required her to stay in the hotel at least one night either en route or coming back. They were on the first and only nonstop flight to Acapulco, Mexico, on Friday, arriving at one-thirty-five in the afternoon. Cynthia could not move into her time-share condo in the Colonio, El Pleamar, until Saturday. Hardy planned to rendezvous with them on Friday afternoon. He reserved a suite at the Holiday Inn in downtown Acapulco on the strip for the one night.

"I think Carel Van Kampen is coming with Hardy. Remember him from three summers ago when we first met him?" Cynthia quizzed Connie while driving.

"Do you think I'd forget that bird? And especially from this last August when he came with Hardy and stayed at my cottage. It's amazing how many phone calls they make. If Hardy wasn't so straight with being president of the bank, and all, I would think he's involved in something weird like international gambling, assuming there is such a thing, and Van Kampen's somehow part of it too." Connie fiddled with the radio buttons.

"Oh, I don't know. I don't think he's such a bird," Cynthia responded, defending him. "All the phone calls always get charged back to Hardy at the bank, so what difference does it make? Hardy's been running off making phone calls since forever, long before Carel came with him to the Lake. I like Carel. His taste is excellent." She paused thoughtfully. "And he spends lots of money," casting a smile at Connie. "When I've seen him over the last couple of years, I've enjoyed him immensely. I just adore the outfits he brought me from

Holland just for this trip to El Pleamar. Connie, you know, I've seen him every time I visited Hardy. Hardy went out of his way to arrange that Carel would be there. Last May when I went out east for Hardy's annual Derby party, Carel and I spent the most wonderful time together. He always brings me the newest European fashions. One of them that I'll wear in Mexico is a two-piece white skirt with a sheer blouse. The skirt has a hem ruffle on the longer side all the way to the crotch. The short side of the skirt is straight hemmed to show off my gold-threaded underpants. Matching strapped high-heeled shoes too, with little white and gold toe ruffles." She giggled. "He thought the look very alluring when I tried it on for him. I couldn't tell anybody Carel and I rendezvoused because of the divorce and all. Hardy helped a lot with arrangements. Carel and I'll be together in El Pleamar, Connie."

Connie grinned to herself. Cynthia surprised her sometimes, but this news she suspected anyway.

"I think you told me the time-share consisted of two bedrooms with two full-sized beds in each. And the living area hosts a queen-sized sofa sleeper. It sounds like there will be more than ample accommodations for everyone," Connie said.

The sun began to rise as they neared Chicago. Looking at Cynthia, Connie could not help but notice her very apparent tan in the dawn's early light, so golden brown.

"You look like you should be returning from Mexico instead of going with that tan. Wow," Connie said. "And that's quite the haircut you have, Cynthia. It's not ordinary at all. I couldn't help but notice it right away. It's really short, kind of like a Mia Farrow or Twiggy out of the sixties. But for you, yeah, it works with your tan, and you're thin enough to pull it off. Yeah, very cool," Connie complimented, observing the look.

"No, no, not the sixties," Cynthia said. She giggled and relished the compliment, thinking she sensed Connie's jealousy. "I saw the new short haircuts in some of the magazines Carel brought me from Holland. The models have short hairstyles right now. I saw haircuts this way in the December issue of a high-class Netherlands magazine called *Red* and in *Margriet*, a fashion magazine from there too. Carel

119

brought them for me. Their trends are so far ahead of us. I can't wait until Carel and Hardy see it." Cynthia lit up, excited, her golden face shining at Connie. "I hope they love it." She giggled. "Gosh, this is the exit for the O'Hare Hilton already." Cynthia said, leaving the toll road.

*****

Cynthia and Connie's American Airlines flight safely touched down at the Acapulco, Mexico International Airport, which was still under construction. After landing, they passed through immigrations and cleared customs.

"Taxi, lady? Take you where you want to go. Good price for you today."

It seemed like a million Mexican taxi drivers swirled around them, soliciting their business. The winner taxied them to the Holiday Inn. Connie immediately began practicing speaking Spanish aloud. She also put herself in charge of money exchange.

"Now aren't you glad I persuaded you to come, Connie? See? I told you. And you're talking Spanish already," Cynthia said as a feeler.

"Hmm, so far, so good," Connie said. *Persuaded?* She shot a quizzical glance at Cynthia and let it drop.

The sparkling Pacific Ocean in Acapulco Bay greeted the two women five hundred feet below the road on the ride to the Holiday Inn.

"What an awesome view," Cynthia said, sightseeing past Connie in the back seat. "I didn't notice it last time with the kids and Toby."

"The Pacific sure has a flourishing aqua color, doesn't it?" Connie softly commented, gazing out her window, too, as the taxi rumbled down the steep mountain to the flat ground on the Acapulco strip. "Balboa named it the Pacifico, meaning passive or peaceful after he crossed the Isthmus of Panama and viewed the calm ocean for the first time."

"You're so smart, Connie," Cynthia said honestly.

Arriving at the Holiday Inn, Carel and Hardy awaited them in the tropical-theme lobby. Hardy gave a warm hug to Connie and planted a huge welcome kiss on Cynthia. Carel and Cynthia exchanged a more passionate embrace.

"Remember Connie from the Lake, Carel?" Cynthia asked.

"Of course," he said, extending his hand. "I stayed at her house, too, in August. We are old friends. It is very good to see you again, Connie."

"Likewise." Connie shook his hand. The "old friends" part did not make sense to her.

"Come on, girls. Carel and I'll grab some of this luggage and show you to the suite. Connie, you're on your own with your extra scuba gear."

Hardy fiddled with the room key and finally got it open, "Hey, this is going to be great," he burst out. He grabbed Cynthia, giving her another spontaneous hug. "You girls hurry and get changed. We'll go eat some Mexican food. Drink some margaritas. No JB and water for me here. It's tequila all the way. Wow. First, let's look at Cynthia with that short new haircut. It's great, fabulous, great." He could barely contain himself, trying to light a cigarette and then pushing up his glasses. Everybody's energy flowed from borrowed adrenaline, from the lack of sleep.

"Your haircut is marvelous, my darling," Carel said. "You know it is the rage now in Europe. Not mediocre at all. On you, it accents every angle of your beautiful face." He placed a light kiss on her full-painted ruby lips.

"Head out for margaritas?" Hardy questioned while observing Carel's approving kiss upon Cynthia. Hardy kept one suitcase packed with his version of summer fun attire and fashionable resort wear. This same suitcase came to The Lake with him every August. Only these clothes were not part of his usual attire. Already changed into a pink and white pinstriped short-sleeved shirt with turquoise Bermuda shorts, he bent over to retie his gleaming white new Nikes. Hardy never changed from wearing calf-high black dress socks. He pulled each one up and straightened it on his milk white leg.

"Slammers." Cynthia giggled. "First, I need to change out of this travel stuff into a little something I brought just for the first night here. I packed it right on the top of my suitcase so it could be ready right away." She smiled, showing her snow-white teeth against her golden tan, and slipped into the bathroom to change.

"Real Mexican food, maybe chicken molé with margaritas will work for me," Connie said. "We can't do any unpacking until tomorrow anyway. I need to change clothes, too, before I roast. Hey, hurry up, Cynthia," she called out toward the bathroom door.

After a full ten minutes, the bathroom door opened. Flowing back into the suite, Cynthia appeared wearing a strapless sundress.

"It's from Carel." She gestured at the dress, moving her hands from her cleavage, down the front to mid-thigh. "Oh Carel," she gushed in delight, "you found a dress the same color as the Pacific for our first night here together."

"And it matches your eyes, my love," he said.

After three pitchers of margaritas to wash down the spicy enchilada de pollo, quesadillas de cazón, and tacos de pescado con salsa mexicana y verde, the four hailed a blue and white VW bug cab for a ride back to Hardy's suite to pass out. Carel sat in the front because he was the biggest.

The next day, Cynthia's time-share became available at noon. In El Pleamar some of the old hotels had just begun renovating into condominiums. Connie, duly impressed with Cynthia's, loved the bedroom Cynthia gave her. The ample window to the west framed the color of the fluorescent-blue Pacific Ocean, etching itself in her memory forever. Carel and Cynthia shared the master suite. In the middle of the living area, Hardy flopped onto the sofa sleeper, claiming it. The electric-blue ocean thirty feet below the time-share's private terraza illuminated Cynthia, already changed into a bikini. She called room service for pina coladas immediately after unpacking. She reclined in her chaise lounge sunbathing now, sipping one. In her other hand she held a magazine from Carel to look through. Carel lay in a lounge by her side. The colors of the fresh-picked tropical flowers in the coconut drink accentuated the brilliant colored flowers in her two-piece suit, a present from Carel.

"Sweetheart, I wonder if I brought enough clothes? I have my tops stacked up on the dresser, arranged by color, waiting to be worn. How could Connie bring just one suitcase, and she even packed some scuba gear in it, too, that she didn't carry on the plane?" Cynthia asked Carel, shaking her head disbelievingly. She put down her magazine and turned onto her side toward Carel. She readjusted her bikini top.

"Do not fret, my love, I will take you shopping later today and again tomorrow," he promised.

"I'll buy another suitcase to take new clothes home in," she said, hanging on to her orange and lime striped CK bikini top this time as she turned onto her flat stomach.

"Hey, where we going for dinner tonight?" Hardy approached the couple, pulling up another lounge chair with one hand, and holding a margarita with a cigarette in the other.

"There's a fantastic Mexican restaurant right here in El Pleamar. I think it's called La Cabana. I remember it from the time before. After we discovered it, we went there for breakfast, lunch, or dinner every day, and sometimes all three. Good drinks, food, and service too. Definitely, you won't get sick from the food there," Cynthia said. "They even have menus in English and take American Express. The waiters try to talk English a little." Smiling at Hardy, she turned, raising herself up on her elbows. "We can walk there. I think you can see it from here if you look over the terraza railing," she said and pointed.

"Great, great." Hardy plunked into his chair and leaned over to adjust his black socks.

"Sounds good to me too," Connie said, dragging another chair over with a beer in her other hand. "The little walk sounds wonderful. Close. I'll like that, especially tonight. I think the traveling caught up with me. I'll stop at that dive shop down the hill that we drove past on the way up here to make arrangements for Monday."

At dinner, Cynthia devoted herself entirely to Carel Van Kampen, not including Hardy or Connie. This made her project herself to Van Kampen with a look that said nothing in the whole wide world—books, music, pictures, even herself—compared to him and his interests. Cynthia saturated Van Kampen with adoring attention.

Connie glanced at Hardy. He looked content watching them. His eyes never left Cynthia in action.

*****

On Monday afternoon, Connie returned to the time-share after a scuba dive excursion to Roquetta Island. She found no one there. She walked lazily out on the terraza again to see if Cynthia lay sunbathing down below at the pool. *Not there. Well,* Connie thought, *she must be shopping with Carel and Hardy is down at the sports bar placing bets.* She stood facing the ocean, sunlight framing her. A strong knock sounded on the door of the time-share. She walked through the cool room and peeked through the peephole. Seeing the young male staff person holding the laundry, she opened the door.

"Su lavado, Senorita."

"Si, lo pone alli, por favor." Connie motioned to the closet. "Y, uno momento." She hurried to find some pesos for a tip. Hardy always threw his change in his notebook on the side table by his sofa sleeper. She opened his notebook to grab some pesos for the tip. She recognized the book as a journal, but did not linger.

"Aqui, Señor, gracias," she said when she returned to the door. She handed a tip to him and closed the door.

Connie could not resist returning to the journal. She opened it.

Friday, February 10

Arrived today. The water looks very tempting. Cynthia will like a swim in the scanty two-piece suit I have brought for her. We'll have a pleasure swim together. How beautiful she will be with me. The sea will be like a miniature lake with tall trees bordering it with green branches dipping into the water. We will be like we were playing "Lady of The Lake" when we were naked children. The sun shining on the feathered spray shows me only your face, Cynthia. How I love you, my darling, cousin. We'll drift forever together. I'll give you all the melange of amber lace clothes and Channel No.2 you love for your gorgeous body. My eyes are dazzled by you, my brain dazed. My fancy is the haunting memory of your splendid eyes lighted with fire and passion. You are beyond my fairest dreams of women. You are vivid, highly colored, and brilliant. You are the pure sweet lily, and the queenly rose together. I say to myself, "I have never seen a face or figure like my dear beautiful cousin Cynthia's." No wonder when we played "Lady of the Lake" as children, you commanded kings and princes at your feet.

"Amazing," Connie murmured to herself, sitting down on a chair by the side table. She pondered what she was reading revealed. "This…oh man," she spoke aloud to no one but herself. She continued reading. She could not stop now.

Saturday, February 11th

You pleased me so last night with the love that shone in your eyes and trembled on your lips. The love in your voice for me would falter and die away. Your love for me is that of a mistress that never fails to fascinate me. I am delighted with just the two of us being here together, my darling Cynthia. My heart is warm with the charm of your words. I say to myself, "there must be no renewal of our childish nonsense of early days." I must be careful not to allude to it. I am a gentleman. I will never exaggerate or say one word I don't mean. Your welcome to me last night most gracious and kind. Your beautiful face softened and changed completely for me.

She glanced toward the terraza to be sure none of them approached it. Then she continued reading.

Sunday, February 12th

*Dinner tonight in the sweet-scented February eve-
ning with just the two of us together, my darling
Cynthia. You wore the dress I gave you. How lovely
you looked in my favorite colors. Amber and white,
a Mexican dress of rich amber brocade trimmed
with white lace against your golden tan. Your
queenly head was circled with diamonds. Jewels
gleamed like fire on your breasts. I saw you as a girl,
but now I say you are simply perfect. As I watch
you, high and brilliant is not enough for you. I am
president of the bank, and there is a large merger
coming. I can give you anything you want. But I
need you in Connecticut close to me. I am making it happen. I will arrange it all for you to marry
Van Kampen in Connecticut. Then you can live
near me. Your charm is magical. I can't help but see
you treat me differently. Your voice takes a different
tone addressing me. Your face takes another expression as though you regard me apart from everyone
else. The dinner was wonderful tonight. When we
rose to go, you stood near me. "Let's not go to the
hotel just yet, Hardy. It's early. Let's walk along the
beach," you spoke in so low a tone of voice that only
I could hear you, my dear cousin and playmate. We
held hands strolling barefoot down the sandy beach
in the moonlight. I carried your shoes. "It seems to
me, Hardy, I have barely exchanged one word with
you yet tonight," you whispered in my ear. "I feel
like we've talked for hours," I returned laughing. "I
forget time when I am talking to the one, to you."
I wondered at the moonlight illuminating your
splendid face. For a few minutes, silence reigned
between us and you were the first to break it. "I
hope to please you," you spoke softly. "You hope to*

please me?" I interrogated. "Whom should I think of, if it's not you, Hardy?" You inquired with both love and reproach in your voice. We sat then in the chairs by the sea. The evening air was clean. It gave the tropical flowers even more fragrance. "Shut your eyes, Hardy. Dream," you murmured tenderly to me, Cynthia. "I shall dream more vividly if I keep them open and look at you," I returned. Then in a few minutes I began to think I must be in dreamland. "Your rich, clear voice, is so soft, so low…it's like a room being filled with the sweetest music," I told you, caressing your hand. "Your voice is like no human voice that I can remember. Its seductiveness and tenderness toward me is irresistible," I confessed to you, Cynthia. I looked at you in the pearly moonlight. No wonder when we were children I bowed before you bearing gifts. The soft moonlight seamed to render your face more beautiful. Your spell was over me. "How wondrously lovely you are," I quietly exclaimed with a flushed face and my heart beating fast. Suddenly, our eyes met, your scarlet lips parted, and my white trembling fingers drew you toward me.

With hesitation and disbelief, Connie tried digesting all this. Hardy's covert obsession with Cynthia shocked her. She remembered a choice cluster of flowers on Cynthia's bodice last night at dinner, which Carel gave her, but no diamonds or jewels. Giving that serious thought, she also knew that she and Hardy caught a cab up to the condo while Carel and Cynthia departed holding hands to stroll along the beach. Later that night, Cynthia and Carel reclined in chaise lounges while the pearly moonlight danced on the ocean. She and Hardy could see them from the balcony over the terraza where they were drinking margaritas, sharing friendly chatter together. Connie marveled at the beauty of the night. She remembered now when Hardy spoke his focus never changed from the couple on the terraza, answering her, but not even turning his head toward her in conversation.

"How did your dive go?" she heard Cynthia's voice as she came up onto the terraza with Carel from the beach below. Connie rapidly shut the journal, pushing it back to its original spot in the center of the side table.

"*Hola*. Good," Connie nervously called back to her, feeling caught. Hurrying out onto the terraza, she quickly rattled on. "The water is incredibly transparent, clear. It becomes colorless underneath it, believe it or not, by the Roquetta Island out there," she said, pointing toward it. "The fish are illuminated like they're dyed or painted, golden yellows, inky blacks, frosted snowy whites—the colors are iridescent. We dove around an old sunken boat, named *Mantarraya* with a cross on it, kind of funky. Roberto, the dive master from Quebec, wants me to go on a night dive. He says that with our dive lights on at night, not only the fish, but also the sea plants and animals become an illuminated spectacle. He describes them as bursting forth, glistening in full view. I think I'll rent an underwater camera if I go."

"Not tonight, I hope," Cynthia interrupted, not caring about the dive description. "Carel already bought us all tickets to go on the pirate cruise boat we see sailing out at night from that pier on the beach past La Cabana. They sail to the island where you dove today. What's its name again, Connie?"

"Roquetta," Connie answered. The three slumped down in onto the comfortable, overstuffed blue lounge chairs provided on the terraza.

"They sure seem to be having fun on that pirate cruise boat. It'll be a riot. You get pirate costumes to put on over your clothes. All you can drink is included with an outdoor barbecue, and a live band at the island," Cynthia said.

"That's okay. I can dive tomorrow night if I decide to go. I'm switching to beer though. I need a break from margaritas. Sounds like fun. Thank you, Carel," Connie said. She made a note to look at him directly while thanking him. "Oh, by the way, the laundry is back and in the closet."

They heard the door bang open. Momentarily, Hardy burst out to the terraza from the room. He possessed the only key while the others used the terraza entrance.

"Hey, I'm back. What's happening?"

"Well"—Cynthia stood up and kissed Hardy on the cheek—"Carel bought tickets for all of us for that pirate cruise we see sailing at night. We get pirate costumes to wear over our clothes."

"A pirate cruise with costumes! We'll need to bring our cameras and take lots of pictures. We'll get to pretend we're pirates?" Hardy enthusiastically asked before he turned around to go back to the refrigerator in the kitchen. He grabbed a Corona from it and lit a cigarette, smiling in anticipation. "A dress-up party in costumes! Does anyone else want a beer? How do they say that, Connie?" he said. He shuffled his feet for a second while smoking in thrilled anticipation. One black sock slid down to his ankle.

"Cerveza. I'll have one too," Connie answered, getting up to go into the refrigerator. "Carel, *una cerveza?*" she asked.

"Yes. I will."

"I'm waiting for the free margaritas tonight. They're included you know," Cynthia chimed in, regaining attention from the other three.

"Oh, you know I'll have margaritas with you tonight, Cynthia. You won't be drinking alone," Hardy assured her, pushing up his glasses with his yellow-stained fingers.

"Slammers." Cynthia giggled and then radiantly smiled. "I have to show you the present Carel bought me," she said when Connie returned. She held out her left hand to exhibit an exquisite ring where she wore her wedding band before. The center hosted a dazzling spotless sapphire. Its magnificence required no small jewels to surround it for emphasis.

"The color matches the blueness of your eyes and the ocean, my darling. Inside we inscribed our initials." Carel doted on her.

"Carel bought it in the jewelry department of the new Sanborns," Cynthia said. "Carel said Sanborns is comparable to a Bloomingdale's or a Macy's in the United States." Still holding her hand out, she said, "It's a caret and it's three-star gem quality authenticated." She paused. "Carel says that's important for insurance," she added with a beholden look to Carel that made him gently kiss her on the ear.

Hardy pushed up his glasses. Taking Cynthia's hand, he riveted his eyes on the azure crowned ring. His heart beat with anticipation. Could this mean his plan for Cynthia moving to Connecticut leaped forward?

"Good choice, Carel," Hardy assured Carel. "You're right about the sapphire matching Cynthia's eyes."

Now Connie's turn came to comment on the ring. "How brilliant a rock it is," she said, not knowing what to say. She thought it totally ostentatious.

*****

The last streams of orange light shone on the terraza as the sun edged toward the western horizon on the Pacific. The water carried the loud Salsa music blaring from the "Merodeador Del Mar" speakers down on the beach for the pirate fiesta to the terraza. Hardy and Carel sipped their beers while waiting for Cynthia and Connie. Carel smoked a Havana and Hardy his usual cigarette. The delicious smell of Channel No. 2 drifted from Cynthia's open bedroom door to the terraza where they sat. Then she floated out to join them. Her pink top sparkled with cranberry sequins spelling out El Pleamar, which matched her two-toned pink and cranberry striped short shorts. Rosita sandals completed the ensemble.

"I guess I won't need my pink sunglasses. It's going to be dark soon. Where is Connie?" Cynthia asked, surprised not to see Connie on the terraza yet. Cynthia always liked to make the last appearance of the group.

"Not out yet." Hardy jumped up to acknowledge her presence first, because of the alluring forewarning smell of the Channel No. 2, one of his presents. "You look like a movie star in that pink with your tan." He pushed up his glasses. The palms of his hands began to sweat just looking at her.

"Thank you, Hardy. What a sweet thing to say." She fluttered her long lashes at him. She already knew it.

Connie finally came out onto the terraza.

"Yes, Connie, you are ready, too, now." Carel turned to greet her

"I needed to put new film in my camera for tonight," she said, holding up her camera.

"Oh, my camera." Hardy quickly put out his cigarette to go grab it from his travel case. He started coughing as he hurried from his chair. "This cough, damn thing," he grumbled.

The reverberating music from the pirate fiesta kept signaling them to come to the boat. Hardy and Connie walked ahead down to the beach. Cynthia and Carel lagged behind when they started on the sand. Carel carried Cynthia's rosita sandals.

Nearly blocked out by the earsplitting music, the drone of the diesel engines vibrated through the hull.

"Cervesa, margarita, slammer, rum," the energetic young crewmember said, welcoming them. "All you drink included in ticket. *Si. Todas las bebidas estan en el pricio de las boletas. Aqui.* Here. Costumes for your clothes. Pirates."

With great excitement, Hardy pulled his on first.

"A costume sure makes you leave your bank in Connecticut, Hardy," Connie joked while putting hers on. She watched him, bouncing from foot to foot, childlike, having a grand time already.

He punched her lightly in the arm, smiling ear to ear. "Help me tie this bandanna on my head," he said.

One of the Mexican crew rushed over to spray margarita into Cynthia's mouth from a look-alike fire extinguisher after she tied her pirate costume on. She tilted her head to the side, parting her pearly-pink-painted lips wide, wallowing in being the center of attention. Hardy pushed forward to take the picture.

"More, more. Do it again," Hardy yelled at the crewman, motioning toward Cynthia. But the barman had already moved toward another *belleze* with the fake fire extinguisher filled with libation.

A short boat ride took them to Roquetta Island. One of the two landings on the island belonged to the Fiesta Company for its tourist industry. The setting sun balanced itself briefly on the horizon of

Pacific and then extended a few lingering orange fingers across the water, mixing with moonbeams sparkling on it.

On the island, enthusiastic servers called out to the partygoers, welcoming them. "All you can eat at barbecue and drink included. *Pollo, pescado, cruedo.*" The blaring music began again, not the boat band this time, but recordings on turntables blasting from a giant group of speakers hanging in the coconut palm trees above the sand. The sweet smell of blossoming mango trees perfumed the night air.

"The limbo stick, the limbo stick," Hardy yelled to Connie and ran to get into the line. Connie jumped in too.

"How low can you go," the record sang out.

"Oh, my gosh. Hardy is still in!" Connie sang with the crowd, clapping, after knocking the stick down. "He's going again. Only two people left! Go, Hardy, go," she yelled at the top of her lungs. Hardy leaned way back, jumping baby steps under the stick. The ties in his red bandanna flopped, glistening with sweat in the moonlight.

"Yeah, you did it! Hardy, you won!" Connie clapped and whistled with the rest of the half-drunk crowd. "Wow. You've won the grand prize. A bottle of tequila."

"What a night, what a night," Hardy exclaimed, splitting his words with coughing. He grabbed Connie, hugging her and almost leaping out of his costume in excitement. Then he looked around for Cynthia and Carel. Too busy, he did not notice their absence until now. He coughed again, holding his chest.

"Hardy? Hardy? Are you okay?" Connie took hold of his arm to steady him during the spell. "I've noticed you coughing a couple of times lately. Are you sure you're okay?"

He shook his head yes, trying to catch his breath.

"Maybe I'm not smoking enough," he tried to joke, shaking his head with another rattling cough. His damp bandanna flew off his head. His black stockings sagged down around his ankles.

Silently, Cynthia and Carel reappeared from the shadows of the palm trees holding hands.

"Hey guys, Hardy won the limbo contest," Connie shouted to them as they approached.

"Yeah, first prize!" Laughing, Hardy held up his bottle of tequila high with gusto.

That night back at the time-share, Hardy and Connie watched the sparkling moonbeams prance on the tranquil Pacific from the terraza above it while sipping their nightcaps. Hardy coughed spasmodically, spilling his tequila.

"Hardy, I really recommend you see your doctor when you're back home," Connie said, shaking her head at him with concern. "Do you feel all right otherwise?"

"Yeah, yeah. I'm fine, I'm fine," he said, lighting a cigarette.

"Well, you don't sound fine to me."

*****

The end of the week inevitably arrived. For dinner the last night they went to La Cabana restaurant one more time on the romantic Pleamar beach.

"Una mesa para quartro personas, por favor," Connie told Fidel, their favorite waiter. "Con una vista del mar."

"Si, si, senorita." Fidel hustled to prepare the table with salsa verde and salsa Mexicana to start, and then take their drink orders. "Algo tomar?" he asked.

"What do you guys want to drink?" Connie said.

"Ah, how do you say beer?" Carol said.

"Margarita and margarita." Hardy motioned to Cynthia and himself.

"Y cerveza, tambien, Pacifico," Connie said. She motioned at Carel. "Dos Pacificos."

"Si."

The four gazed at the beach and sea for the last time in the late afternoon sun. Mexican families played with their children in the warm water. Beach dogs trotted by hoping to find a morsel of food dropped in the sand. Fishermen came ashore with their day's catch to sell to the restaurants along the beach. Another day in El Pleamar peacefully washed back into the Pacific.

Fidel smartly handed the group three menus in English and one to Connie in Spanish.

"Our last night, I'm so sad. What should I order, Carel?" Cynthia leaned her head on Carel's arm with moist eyes.

"Not to worry, my love," Carel said. He tenderly patted her hand. "I will bring us to this beautiful El Pleamar again."

*****

Cynthia and Connie departed first for Chicago the following morning. Hardy and Carel went early to the airport to see them off with tender kisses and hugs. All the sweet goodbyes made Connie numb. After a smooth nonstop American Airlines return flight back to O'Hare, the two women checked into their room for the night at the Hilton.

"No slammers here, so I think I'll order some champagne. Mumms, maybe. Connie, I'll just duck into the bathroom to change. I'm going to put on my strapless turquoise dress from Carel in honor of our first night in El Pleamar," Cynthia said. She picked up the phone for room service.

Two bottles of the chilled bubbly arrived. Cynthia came back into the room wearing the strapless dress that matched the dazzling sapphire ring and her blue eyes. She moved her hand forward to Connie, enabling them both to see the ring better. She softly whispered, "It's an engagement ring, and Hardy is going to do all the arranging so the wedding can be in Connecticut. Let's toast to Carel and me," Cynthia said. She popped the cork and poured the bubbling liquid into the two frosted goblets. They clinked their glasses. Cynthia chugged down her first and poured a second glass.

"Here you finish this bottle," Cynthia said to Connie. "I'm opening the other, and there is more where that came from." She stood up and dragged the phone toward the bathroom, clutching the other bottle of Mumms and chilled champagne glass in her hand. Grabbing the doorknob, she turned back to Connie and said in a muffled voice, "I must call Reginald. I need to tell him."

CHAPTER 10

Husband and Wife

July 1980, Hartford, Connecticut

"This is Harden Alden over at the First National of Connecticut Bank. Would you put me through to Judge Whitman, please?"

"Yes, Mr. Alden." Harden frowned at the piped music he heard during the brief wait.

"Judge Whitman," the judge answered the phone.

"Jerry, Hardy here. What's your schedule after you're finished today? Thought we could have a couple of drinks at the club. There's something I want to ask you about."

"Sure, sure. I'll be ready for a cocktail by later today. Say five-thirty or so, Hardy?"

"Good, great. See you there."

The two men frequently met at the Emerald Links Country Club after their business days concluded. That evening, they shook hands first and then comfortably planted themselves in padded stools with armrests at the classic older-style wooden bar. The warm wood interior of the barroom, complete with huge ceiling beams and a massive central stone fireplace extending up to and through the roof line, welcomed the club members.

"What will you have, Judge?" the pretty female bartender asked. "I already have Mr. Alden's JB and water. I just love how he never switches." She smiled at Hardy.

"Sapphire, splash of tonic."

"Put it on my account please," Hardy said. "Good to see you, Jerry."

"Likewise." The bartender delivered the drinks. They each took a healthy swallow. "So what's the good news from you?"

"Well, here is what I wanted to ask your opinion about," Hardy began, lighting a cigarette. "My cousin, out in Wisconsin, finalized her divorce in April. She sold her home very quickly and is already in the process of buying a house here. She likes the one on Carpenter Lane, not too far from me. Do you know that one? She wants to marry this fellow from Amsterdam, Carel Van Kampen. I've dealt with him through the bank. He traveled with me, ah, several years ago for the first time to Wisconsin when I always go in August. He has returned with me every year since then and when I go in the fall for my birthday too. He and my cousin fell madly in love at first sight."

Hardy chuckled and took a chug of his Jim Beam. Then he drew hard on his cigarette. Coughing, he reluctantly ground it into the ashtray.

"Have to stop smoking these things one of these days," he mumbled. "Anyway, my gut feeling is he is shady. Not on the up-and-up, if you know what I mean. Wouldn't doubt if he's hooked up with the Dutch Mafia. But I've nothing to stop the bank from dealing with him. With my cousin's recent divorce, I feel like I need to watch after her a little bit. They plan to get married in the house she is proposing to buy, a few months after the closing. She must wait six months to remarry. Wisconsin laws, or they would probably get married sooner. Pretty quick by my standards. I don't really trust this guy." Hardy paused and noted that the judge's reaction seemed interested and agreeable.

Jerry took a swallow of his Sapphire. He nodded his head with a positive slow up-and-down motion. He rubbed the bottom of his chin with his left forefinger, drawing his lips back together in thought. He waited for more information.

"I thought I'd ask you to do me a little favor for the family," Hardy quickly continued. "I thought if you performed the marriage ceremony in the house, like they want, you could possibly forget to file the marriage papers for a while, until things look okay. Maybe the guy won't even stick around. What do you think?"

Judge Whitman listened to crazier requests than this during his career. Sometimes with substantial payoffs. This little favor for his friend and associate didn't hold a candle to other propositions he encountered. He knew Hardy Alden well. Cripes, they belonged to the same club together. He could sure understand Hardy's concern for his cousin.

"She is the sister I never had," Hardy had told him several times.

"At my age my memory is terrible anyway," the judge said, laughing. "I could easily forget to file the marriage certificate for a while or forever for that matter. When it progresses to a point for a license, Hardy, send them to me for that too. Without charge."

"Thanks, Jerry. The family thanks you too." Hardy extended his hand to the judge to shake on the deal. "Time for another round?"

"Sure, sure," Judge Whitman said, raising his empty glass.

Hardy motioned to the bartender and repeated, "On my bill. Please."

*****

The first thing the next morning Hardy called Cynthia in Wisconsin to tell her about his meeting with Judge Whitman. He held a cigarette but did not light it. He remembered the horrifying third appointment yesterday when he met with his doctor in the morning before going to the bank. He threw out all the medications and cried. He needed to talk to Cynthia with this good news about Judge Whitman before the scheduling nurse called him with the appointment dates to the recommended specialist. He would begin to groom Mitchell to act as president of the bank immediately in his absence during treatment. Mitchell would welcome the opportunity.

He would assume if his older brother gave him the chance to show his competence of the responsibility of being bank president, Hardy was thinking about retiring.

"Morning, Hardy here, Cynthia, I have some great news," Hardy said, calling from his phone in his office.

"Hardy, hi, good morning."

"I'm calling to tell you I met with my friend, Judge Whitman, at the club after the bank closed yesterday. He said he will be glad to marry you in your new house here if that's what you still have in mind."

"Oh, Hardy. Oh, yes. Thank you. I thought it such a wonderful idea ever since you first suggested it," Cynthia answered gratefully.

Later that afternoon Cynthia finished preparing a light dinner for herself and the kids. Having a little time until they would eat, she decided to call Connie with the news.

"Hi, Connie, it's Cynthia. I'm just calling to tell you my house here really is sold. I'm so relieved it sold so quickly, and so lucky to have Hardy making arrangements to close on the house in Connecticut."

"Hi, yeah, this really is fast. But your house is so beautiful and, with your swimming pool—well, I guess it doesn't surprise me too much."

"Thanks. Anyway, Connie, as soon as the date for the closing in Hartford is set, Carel and I'll know the date for the wedding. We plan to be married by a judge friend of Hardy's and stay in the house that night. What do you think, Connie? Will you come and be my maid of honor? Hardy is the best man."

"Of course, I will. I'd be very glad too," Connie slowly replied. A chill crept up her spine as she remembered Hardy's journal.

"Oh, good, I'm so glad."

Cynthia no more than hung up the phone and it rang.

"I've got the closing date, I've got the date," Hardy excitedly announced the news to Cynthia from the other end. "It's July 29."

"Oh, my gosh. It's sooner than I thought it would be. Oh, thank you, Hardy, thank you. You'll take care of communicating everything to Carel when you deal with him from the bank, please? Like usual?"

"Yes, yes, and I'll keep you updated on everything too. Right now, we need to work on your financial holdings to be transferred to my bank so I can help you here where you will be living. Makes sense, doesn't it, Cynthia?" he asked.

"Of course, and I trust you completely. It's just that I've never taken care of the finances. Toby always did. You'll have to help me a lot."

"We'll see how much we can take care of by phone, Cynthia. I may have to fly out there earlier in August for my annual visit. Maybe the first week, right after the closing to get everything in order. Maybe we can fly back together. I'll see what I can schedule."

"That would be terrific. How can I ever thank you enough?"

August 20, 1980, The Move

The moving van arrived first at Cynthia's new house on Carpenter Lane in Hartford. Cynthia and her children followed in her DCM van two days later. She and Hardy picked an October 12 wedding date, exactly six months from her divorce. She needed to settle into the house and start the children in their school right away. After Cynthia's telephone service began the next day, she called Connie later in the afternoon to update her.

"We'll get married at the house like we talked about. The ceremony is going to be small, just the four of us, the judge, plus my two little angels and Amber, my niece," she told Connie. "I still must make a lot more preparations, but it's just spectacular the way Hardy helped plan everything out here. He even made reservations at the country club for a reception after the ceremony. But you know what, Connie? I still haven't bought my wedding dress."

"You better hurry up on that. They'll probably be coming out with the spring collections soon," Connie cautioned her.

"Well, I figured a trip to Macy's in New York would solve the dress dilemma. Hardy said he would take me and make the reservations ahead for a personal bridal consultant. He said Amber could stay with Rebecca and Samuel. Hardy's ex-wife lives a couple blocks from me and will check on the kids to be sure that everything is okay. He wants to take me to dinner in New York and stay overnight. He said he is going to buy me a new dinner dress because it is a special occasion. I'm so excited and glad we're going together."

"It sure seems like Hardy is doing so much to help on the Connecticut end, you'll only have yourself and the kids to worry about," Connie said in a matter-of-fact way. But her pug nose crinkled up in apprehension.

*****

Carel arrived from Holland four days before the October wedding in plenty of time to meet with the judge for the license. Cynthia had made the appointment for the necessary blood work appointment too. Together with Cynthia in her new house, he held her face gently on both sides and kissed her sensuous painted lilac lips

"Yes, my darling, not to worry. We will leave tomorrow by nine o'clock after the children go to school. Connie's flight will arrive at eleven in the morning. There will be plenty of time to collect her from the plane. You fixed the house so beautiful. Like you," Carel said. He kissed her luscious lilac lips again for a long moment. "For tomorrow I have made reservations at Panache, the restaurant Hardy recommended for the four of us. He said it is traditional in your country, the night before the wedding, the groom's dinner."

"Yes, the rehearsal dinner." Her azure eyes sparkled.

"I have some extra money now, so I can spend."

"Oh, Carel, I've noticed how generous you are since you've been here," she said, looking up into his bottomless black eyes in appreciation. "The dress and accessories you brought me are all the rage. I'll wear them tonight." She snuggled against him. "You give me my own way entirely. I'm so happy." Then suddenly she withdrew her hand from his touch.

"I am sorry, my darling. Are my hands cold?" He kissed her on the forehead to apologize.

After the groom's dinner at Panache, Carel and Hardy returned Cynthia and Connie to Cynthia's house.

"I don't know why Carel wanted to stay at Hardy's tonight instead of here. He's stayed there every night since he arrived," Cynthia complained to Connie.

"Looks to me like he wants the wedding night to be special, so appreciate it," Connie scolded her while Cynthia paced restlessly back and forth.

"I think we'll open one of the bottles of Mumms that Hardy brought for after the ceremony. What do you say, Connie?"

"I say good," Connie said. She nodded her head and rubbed her fingertips hard across the insides of her palms.

"Take a couple of the hollow-stem champagne glasses out. They're in the etched glass china cabinet, Connie, not the other cabinet. They bubble better. I like the bubbles tickling my nose. I'll grab a bottle from the back fridge."

Cynthia paused at each child's door to check on the sleeping angels as she passed their doorways. She left the nightlight on in Rebecca's room because Connie shared it for the weekend.

Connie walked over to the beautiful china cabinet that originally came from Europe to adorn Golden Bounty. Cynthia had procured it for herself. Cynthia knew its worth as she had it and other priceless furnishings she owned from her great-grandparents appraised. She wanted to be surrounded by the rich beauty of the original antique furnishings. Connie stepped back to Rebecca's piano bench, gingerly placing the goblets in two crystal silver coasters atop the baby grand. Cynthia returned with the champagne, popped it open, and began to pour.

"I feel such a strange indifference from you about this wedding, although you're so light and bubbly," Connie spoke gently. She sat still while her friend paced.

"Here's to strange indifference," Cynthia proposed the toast. She and Connie both took several swallows in silence. Cynthia, now standing by the piano, opened and closed the key cover again.

"I hate this disgusting dress. It's gaudy," Cynthia said with loath. She picked up several magazines from the coffee table and set them down again. Her eyes fell upon the book Connie brought along to read.

"What book is that?" she asked

"*Lady of Lions*," replied Connie.

Cynthia raised it and then sat down on the black leather davenport, a gift from Natty.

"I wonder where Natty got the money for this expensive sofa?" she said absently, still holding the book. Clutching *Lady of Lions* as if in a trance, she turned some pages, pausing to take a sip of her champagne. "Pour some more, Connie," she said.

Connie topped the gold-rimmed goblets, with the etched lions, and then sat sipping her champagne without a word. When fifteen minutes passed, with a strange smile on her lips, Cynthia stood up from the sofa and laid the book down.

"I have figured it out at last," she said.

"Figured what out?" Connie asked.

"I can be like a lady of lions." She pressed her lips tight together with the corners turned upward, her smile still half there. "I can be a lady of lions guarding over myself and my children with Carel's money, like the lions guarding Golden Bounty for my great-grandmother, Agatha. I have my youth, beauty, and wit," Cynthia answered with her fingers wrapped tight around her champagne goblet. "With Carel I don't have to worry. Our needs are very amply provided for. And I believe he truly loves the children. That's important. My children have expensive taste too. I'm still not sure what he does, but that's inconsequential, and why should I care? I just have to stay focused on my own wants and needs, making no allowance for affections."

"You mean affection for Reginald, don't you?" Connie said to let her know she understood.

October 12, The Wedding

The wedding day seemed as though Mother Nature herself did her utmost to help make it brilliant. Wedding presents arrived from Cynthia's Aunt Natty. Hardy's younger brother Mitchell and family, along with the judge's wife, would be part of the celebration at the country club.

"Your house decorations for the wedding are perfect. You did such a lovely job," Connie sincerely complimented Cynthia, helping her slip into the blue-gray dress in the afternoon before the four o'clock wedding. "Your eyes are so open and alert looking," Connie said, admiring her friend's youthful face. "The dress is gorgeous on you, making you more beautiful than you already are."

Cynthia played her part in the scene bravely.

"Do you know what I did? Before my trip back to New York for my dress fitting, I scheduled an appointment with Dr. Rool Ool, a revolutionary new facial plastic surgeon. Aunt Natty knew about him from some of her cronies. Rool Ool specializes in treating age-related under-eye puffiness. He fills in the flat spots below the puffy area. Then it creates an illusion of a more open eye. The whole procedure only took two hours. No bruising like the old-fashioned eyelift. I walked out of the clinic looking like this with no discomfort. Carel told me not to even think about the cost. Oh, Connie, I need to always remember how lucky I am to have him."

"Wow. No wonder your eyes look so brilliant. Here, let me put the cap on your dress. The darker gray tint in it accentuates your blue eyes even more. And I think your choice of the pale yellow chrysanthemums for your bridal bouquet is just right, wonderful for autumn too."

"The cap is silk taffeta to match the wide-hem finish of the gown at the floor," Cynthia added, admiring her reflection in the floor-length mirror.

"And the basic dress, so classic and flattering. Strapless so the cap fits perfectly. Beautiful, just beautiful," Connie said, approving her friend's reflection.

"The sapphire earrings are from Hardy. He said for 'something blue' and to express sensuality and fun as well. Dear, sweet Hardy." Cynthia touched her hand to her earlobe. "And the something old and borrowed is a white antique lace handkerchief tucked in my bodice from Natty." She swallowed hard. "Oh, I can't cry. I'll ruin my face."

*****

Judge Whitman stood in front of the fireplace in Cynthia's house facing Carel and Cynthia. Connie stood on Cynthia's side, as did Hardy next to Carel. Carel stood tall, wearing a black Giorgio Armani morning coat with long tails. The toes of his patent leather shoes shined beneath his pinstriped gray-black morning trousers. A classic silk cummerbund held his stark white pleated shirt snug. His charcoal eyes relaxed and embraced Cynthia. His hands, folded in front, showed his manicured fingernails. Hardy wore a navy blue Brooks Brothers suit he would wear to the bank. He added a bright pink tie for the special occasion. Connie decided upon a neutral buffed lemon tailored dress when she learned the color for the bridal bouquet, not to detract from Cynthia in any manner. As it turned out, her dress enhanced the pale butter color of the chrysanthemums in the bouquet, making them look more vibrant. The three excited children managed to stand quiet looking on. Amber and Rebecca clasped each other's hand in anticipation, not wiggling. Samuel tried hard to keep from shuffling his feet.

"You must try hard to stand very still for a few minutes while the judge is talking." Cynthia had told them earlier.

Cynthia turned toward them now and blew them a kiss. Carel nodded his head and smiled at them. The girls wiggled involuntarily.

The brief ceremony commenced. The judge babbled a few obvious matrimonial words. He and Hardy had shared a couple of cocktails before the event. He concluded with "I pronounce you man and wife. You may kiss your lovely bride." He smiled in approval to them. Hardy and Connie clapped and cheered. The kids bounced up and down, clapping, and rushed to kiss Mom. Carel hugged them fondly. "Let's go over to the table, sign the papers to make it all official so the party can begin," the judge said.

"Where do I sign?" Hardy fought hard the urge to cough. "Connie, you're next." He handed her the pen. "As the best man of this grand affair, I've prepared a special toast. The glasses are frosting and the Mumms chilling to castle temperature. The kids will help bring the trays in."

After the certificate signing, Hardy and the children hurried to the kitchen. He carried the tray back with the Mumms and a bottle of nonalcoholic bubbly for the youngsters into the room. Amber, Rebecca, and Samuel gingerly trailed behind him, each carrying a tray with frosted hollow-stemmed crystal champagne goblets on it to set on the dining room table. His hands trembled as he poured, spilling some of the effervescent liquid.

"Here, here, glasses up," he said, smiling broadly at Cynthia. "As Cynthia and Carel's best man, I ask you to join me in a toast to the newlyweds. Actually, I have no idea why I'm called the 'best man' because as far as I know, no one pays the least bit of attention to a man in my position. You hear comments like isn't the bride absolutely radiant, and you are, Cynthia," he said, looking with stark affection in his eyes at Cynthia. "But do you hear anyone ever say 'Wow, have you noticed the best man? Isn't he a great-looking guy?' Noooooo." Everyone politely chuckled. "Actually, I want you all to know I've been an outstanding best man. Who else could calm Cynthia's nerves the way I did? Who else could be such a wise counselor? Who else could be such a reassuring voice in both Cynthia's and Carel's ears? Actually, now that I think about it, with these outstanding qualities, I can't help but wonder why I'm still single?" An amused laugh came from the group. "Seriously, it is a special privilege to offer the first toast to Cynthia and Carel. Let's drink to love. Down the hatch to a striking match."

Everyone raised his or her goblet to take a swallow from it.

"Thank you, thank you, Hardy, my friend. And all my friends here, thank you," Carel said. "Now Cynthia and I will toast to you." Everyone raised their goblets and drank again. "When we are finished here, we must go to join the others at the bar at the Country Club for drinks before dinner. The dinner is at seven o'clock."

*****

Just before the midnight hour Carel drove the van home from the reception with his new wife resting beside him. He parked. Carel turned to his beautiful wife, cooing, "I love you."

"I want air. Don't come near me!" Cynthia stretched out her hands, waving them wildly in front of her face as though beating off pesky wasps.

"My love, you are overcome by the excitement of the day," Carel attempted to soothe her as he would a child. He squeezed her hand. "My darling, inside the house you must rest," he said. He kept his voice steady. He flung open his car door and rushed to her side of the car. She pushed her door open. He grabbed her arm to steady her on the walk to the entrance. Inside the foyer she peeled herself out of her pretty wedding dress. It fell into a crumpled heap on the floor. She drooped onto the leather davenport just inside the living room in her silk underwear.

Her blonde hair, now longer than at El Pleamar, fell around her tan neck carelessly. She artistically arranged it herself, attempting to make it look longer. Carel watched her while she drifted in and out of sleep. He pulled the antique-colored afghan off the back of the davenport to cover her.

"Your beautiful face is flushed, my darling," he whispered. "Your scarlet lips are trembling as though you are a grieving child. I hear you murmuring some words in your sleep, my love. Are you calling my name?"

Suddenly she held out her arms and in an unforgettably forlorn voice cried, "Oh, I'll always love you. I love you so!"

He took it she meant him. Down on his knees by her side he covered her hands with his kisses. "My darling, you are better now. You alarmed me, Cynthia. I thought you ill. My darling, talk to me, please, with a smile," Carel begged.

She opened her eyes a little and sat up halfway on one elbow. Looking at him she remembered that she was now Mrs. Carel Van Kampen, wife of this generous Dutchman who knelt by her side. She sat all the way up and leaned forward, putting her hands on his, and regained control of herself in a split second.

"Oh, Carel. I'm so sorry I alarmed you. I did feel ill, but I'm better now. I'm quite well in fact. Come here," she said. She patted the cushion beside her.

"I'm so glad. Too much excitement of the day," he said. Sitting beside her now, he stroked the top of her hand, assuring her again.

"I'm ready to begin my new life with you now, Carel," she said. She knew the sooner she began it the better. She cuddled into Carel's arms, kissing him on his chin, making herself irresistible to him.

"I am in ecstasy over you, Cynthia," he whispered softy in her ear. "Yes, we will begin our new life together."

As always he continued to make his lengthy trips back to Holland. Hardy welcomed his absences, entertaining her, and available whenever she called him. Sometimes when Carel returned, he thought he found his wife less loving and tender of heart than he believed her to be. But he made no complaints.

"She is so gifted with the house and the children," he told Hardy. "Maybe if I am lucky there could be a third child. I cannot expect everything. I know that she loves me, although she does not say much about it." He adored her, and she accepted his adoration. "She does nothing wrong in my eyes. Everything she says to me is true and right. Everything she does, I proclaim perfect."

Cynthia laid out a luxurious, comfortable life for herself and the children with Carel's continuous money upon his returns from Amsterdam.

"Oh, Carel," she would say to him upon his return. "I'm the happiest woman of all." However, when he would leave again and alone at night, she sobbed because a cloud by the name of Reginald hung over her. "Reginald, Reginald," she called his name. How drastically she missed that man, depressing her all the time. This summer of 1981, Mrs. Carel Van Kampen would not be going to The Lake. She could not believe how wonderful Hardy's words sounded when he told her "I just don't see how I can get away in August to go to The Lake this summer. Way too much work at the bank." At least he would be here with her.

1982, Spring

Carel spent the entire month of March with his wife and children in Hartford. When March ended, he told Cynthia at breakfast, "It is time for me to return to Holland for business. I need to go now, so I am sure to be here for the Kentucky Derby in May. Hardy wants me to be sure."

*****

"Hardy, it's two weeks since Carel called. It's never this long. I'm very worried," Cynthia said. She confided in Hardy, calling him at the bank.

"Nothing at the bank either," Hardy answered, lighting a cigarette. Then he put it out, knowing it could start the hacking cough. "Dinner tonight?" he added.

"That would be nice," she gladly responded.

"I'll call Nan and stop for Amber before I pick you up. I'll admit I'm eager for another dinner with you. It's been a week. I need to take you out more often when Carel disappears to Holland so you're not so lonesome. Will you wear one of the outfits I gave you?" he added. Hardy's dreams became utopia when she wore one of his gifts.

At the club, they sat at the bar first before going to their table for dinner.

"Let's order something to drink here first. What would you like, Cynthia?" he asked.

"A white wine would be good. Is there some way you can follow up on Carel from the bank?" Cynthia questioned. She began to continue the earlier phone conservation.

"Possibly, possibly. I'll see what I can do tomorrow. But tonight let's enjoy our drinks and dinner together," Hardy said. He tilted his head slightly back and peered at her for a long moment from behind his black horn-rimmed glasses. He could not hide his adoring gaze. "You're wearing the coral blue dress that I gave you the last time Carel left the country."

"I adore the large white flower prints in it. It's so tasteful," she said. Her closed lips turned up at the corners. She rested her head on the top of her hand, giving him direct eye contact. He liked to buy ensembles in shades of blue, hoping for a come-hither look from her azure eyes.

"You look lovely in that dress, Cynthia. You know I'm always thrilled when you wear one of the outfits I give you. And the scent of the Channel No. 2, how it penetrates the air," he said. He breathed deep without coughing and sighed like he had just climaxed. Their eyes locked again. He lifted her tanned hand and kissed it.

*****

At five o'clock in the afternoon the next day, Rebecca answered the ringing phone.

"Rebecca, hi, it's Hardy. How are you today, honey? And was school fun?"

"Hi, Uncle Hardy. I'm very well, thank you. Today was picture day at school. We were excused from our regular class schedule to have our pictures taken. I wore a pretty new purple flowered dress that Mother bought me. I think the other girls were jealous. How are you?"

"I'm fine, dear, fine. Is your mother at home?" he asked.

"She's here, but she's in the bathroom dyeing her hair. I'll go see if she can come to the phone."

"Thank you, dear, thank you." Hardy lighted a cigarette.

"Hello." Cynthia came to the phone with a towel wrapped around her head.

"Hi, Cynthia. I have information about Carel. I already talked to Nan. I'll pick up Amber after work and bring her to stay with the children. We need to talk together. We'll go to the club. I'll arrange for a private table there."

"Hardy, what is it, what is it?" She felt a strange chill.

"I'll see you in an hour. We'll talk then."

"Okay, I'll hurry to finish my dye job. You caught me dyeing my hair, but I can be ready."

Hardy arrived at her house with Amber well within the hour.

"Hi, Hardy. Hi, Amber. Amber, everything is ready for you and the kids for dinner in the back fridge. We'll be back earlier than last night," Cynthia greeted her with a warm smile.

It's okay. My mom said I should just stay over again in Rebecca's room. I've got all my school books with me for tomorrow," Amber said. Cynthia kissed all three children as they left. She fondly messed Reginald's son's hair.

At the club, Hardy looked at her squarely from across the table.

"This is what I've found out. Interpol's arrested Carel for racketeering."

"What's Interpol, and what does racketeering mean?" she interrupted, terrorized by the word *arrested*. "Do you mean he's in jail?"

"Cynthia, it's worse than just jail. Interpol is the International Police. Racketeering means he possibly ran gambling, bet fixing, drugs, prostitution—all, or some of it, and maybe more. Maybe he's involved with the Dutch Mafia. I don't know. I can't get any more information than this now. You must realize I have to be careful not to show any personal involvement to Interpol with him because of the bank. I do know this, my dear Cynthia, Carel Van Kampen will not be coming back," he told her with stern finality, holding her trembling hand. He let go to take a large swallow of his JB. He held in check the urge to light a cigarette.

She became so unlike herself—absent, brooding, almost sullen. The smiles, the animation, the vivacity, the wit that distinguished her vanished. She silently drank her wine and spun the bottom of the empty glass.

"Are you going to be ill?"

"No." Her blue eyes raised to his and showed a depth of pain. "Order me another wine, please. What do you mean he won't be coming back?" she managed to ask, shaking her pretty head with her mouth open. "I wish he hadn't gone from the depths of my heart. I wish that," she said, half laughing, with no music in her voice.

"That's what I said and mean, Cynthia. Carel is arrested and will not be coming back. You need to try hard to realize it. I'll do everything I can to help you and make it easier for you."

"I'm confused right now, Hardy. Forget the wine. I need to go home."

"Yes, Cynthia, yes, we'll go."

1982, End of May

After the kids came home from school, changed clothes, and hurried outside to play, Cynthia opened a bottle of Mumms. She poured herself a full goblet to the brim. She held it so the bubbles tickled her nose before taking a large swallow. The she hit the speed dial on her portable phone. Hardy answered after the second ring.

"Hardy, I've made some decisions and need to talk to you," she said.

"I have something for you too. I'll come over, straight from the bank." He coughed.

"Hardy, why do you even try to smoke, and why haven't you seen a doctor?"

She spoke to him as if he were a naughty child. She knew nothing, like everyone else, that he had already met with his doctor more than once before she even moved out to Connecticut. He did not confide to a single soul about his treatments with the recommended specialist.

"Oh, it's nothing. See you in a while," he said.

He arrived at her house shortly. She mixed him a JB and water and topped off her champagne. They sat comfortably in the breakfast nook off the kitchen. Cynthia stated flatly to Hardy, "I'm putting the house on the market. As soon as it is sold, I'm moving back to Port Michigan. I need to go back, to go forward again. I'm dizzy here. Hopefully the house will sell fast so I can get back to buy a house there and get settled before school starts. I'll buy something modest with the proceeds here."

"I think that's a good choice, Cynthia." In fact, he felt relieved to hear her decision, knowing his health situation now. He wished for no one to know. Definitely not her. He observed her from behind his horn-rimmed glasses. She seemed less tanned than usual and fancied her thinner too. The thinner shape of her figure made him smile. He liked it. "This is a good house you own now. It should sell fast." He paused and sipped. "I ran into Judge Whitman last night, and he got back to me already. I have what I think is good news for you. I enlightened him on your situation to see if he could express an opinion. You won't believe this. He could not find any record of your marriage license. Somebody didn't file your license, and there is no certificate anywhere. He doesn't even know how it could happen, but you're not married." Hardy watched Cynthia's mouth open and her face brighten in surprise.

"I'm not married, Hardy? I'm not married?" She leaned forward, hugging herself in jubilation.

"Yes, it's a fact."

"Good God, I'm not, I'm not, I'm not?" She began to giggle hysterically. "I need some champagne, Hardy," she said, tilting her head back and covering her eyes with her hands, laughing.

In double-quick time he hurried to grab a chilled bottle from the fridge. He popped it open and poured a glass for her, hoping she'd calm down. She took a couple of major chugs.

She sat back in her chair. "Stay for dinner, Hardy. Please, stay for dinner."

"I have a huge day coming up at the bank tomorrow and need to go right home tonight. You know I hate to refuse your company, but I have to. I'm feeling a little tired too."

"I understand. It's okay," she said. "I can't believe I'm not married," she exclaimed again, resting her head on her hand, smiling at him. "Not married." She gazed into the distance as if seeing a brighter world there.

*****

The next day, Cynthia listed the house with the same real estate agent she bought it from. Immediately she started packing. Taking a break after lunch, she called Connie. She unloaded the whole story and concluded, "So I need to fly out to look for a house."

"Let me know when. You can stay with me. I'll pick you up. Say, Cynthia, is Hardy still coughing so much? He worries me."

"Yes, yes, he's still coughing. It's much worse than at the wedding. He doesn't smoke anymore. Just lights a cigarette, holds it, and rubs it out in the ashtray. I keep encouraging him to go to his doctor, but he won't listen," Cynthia answered, irritated just thinking about Hardy's cough. Her lips showed a firm disapproval line. "Thanks for offering to pick me up, but I need to rent a car. I'll take you up on the offer to stay with you. Maybe we can get up to the Lake for a day or two. It would probably do wonders for my psyche." She paused. "I'm going to get back to my tasks here. I'm trudging up to the attic now. There isn't much up there to pack, and work my way down. Thanks again, Connie, I'll get back to you as soon as I make the plane reservation. Bye."

"Okay. Sounds good. Bye," Connie said.

Cynthia reclaimed two empty boxes from the garbage and climbed the stairs to the third floor. Flicking on the one overhead light, she saw only three containers stored in the empty space. She walked to the first one to see if anything up there would be worth packing and moving. She tripped on a loose floorboard. A corner of shiny cloth poked out from under the board. She reacted to it like being pulled by a bungee cord snapping back into place, losing her balance. Recovering, she kicked aside the loose board. Amazed, she saw packets laid beneath it in a row, with Dutch writing on every one. Carefully opening up one, she found what she recognized instantly as guilders, Dutch money. She counted twenty packets, each not bigger than a pocketbook. Continuing to investigate the packets, each contained three thousand guilders. Cynthia recoiled at the implications. For a moment, she sat frozen to the floor. Then she tightened her shoelaces as if to get a better grip on it all.

"I need to call Hardy right away," she said to the empty attic. She hustled down the stairs to the phone. She hit the speed dial. "Hardy, Hardy, I need to see you after you've finished today, please. I have something show to you."

He sensed the urgency in her tone. "Okay, okay, I planned on taking Amber to dinner, but instead I'll bring her to your house. She won't mind. You sound apprehensive. What's going on?"

"I'll tell you when I see you later," she said. She sighed with relief knowing he would come as soon as he could.

When Hardy arrived with Amber, the children ran outside to play. She mixed Hardy his JB and water plus poured herself white zinfandel. They settled themselves at the dining room table. She gripped the stemmed wineglass in her hands as she finished telling Hardy about the odd finding, including every detail, down to the exact amount of guilders.

"That's sixty thousand guilders," she said. "How much American money is that, Hardy?" she asked. She set down the wineglass on the white lace tablecloth and leaned forward in eager anticipation.

He contemplated, swallowed some JB and water, and lighted a cigarette, placing it in the ashtray. "Roughly $30,000 dollars."

"That's wonderful," she said. She shot him an intent yet calm stare. For a moment silence hung in the room. Her painted lips parted. "Can you exchange it?" Her central spine tingled.

"No," he answered flatly. "Too much risk in laundering that amount. Offshore investing, to be polite. The best I could possibly do is to replace it with a material object, like a car, say." He paused, studying her, and putting out the burning cigarette. "Volvo bought DAF, the Dutch Auto Firm in Holland so they can sell more Volvos there. They make a coupe with a sunroof. I think it's called a 142. You're still driving that DMC van."

"I'm planning on selling that heap after the move back," she interrupted. "I just don't need it for me and the two kids. It's totally not practical. Tell me about this coupe. Sounds neat. With a sunroof?"

He gazed at her, imagining her sitting next to him in the coupe on a navy blue leather seat. He could see her blue eyes shining only at him. The azure sky above would blow soft air in from the open sunroof, gently tossing her blonde hair back and revealing her beautiful face.

"I'll look into what I can do."

*****

Hardy did his homework on the coupe. He set his alarm, calculating the time change to Rotterdam. Then he dozed fitfully on the sofa. The alarm went off. Hardy placed the call. "Is there someone who speaks English?" Hardy inquired of the person answering the telephone at the Rotterdam Volvo car dealership.

"Yes, yes, sir, I speak English."

"My name is Harden Alden. I'm the president of First National Bank in Hartford, Connecticut, the United States. I'm interested in purchasing a new 142 Coupe, white with sunroof, dark blue leather interior. What are the availability, shipping time frame, and cost?" No one knew he planned to leave for New York Wednesday afternoon and take the red eye to Rotterdam overnight. He planned to act as a character witness for Carel Van Kampen early Friday morning. "I'll be in Rotterdam this Friday," Hardy told the Dutchman on the other end of the line.

"The 142 is aboud $15,000 or 30,000 guilders. Vet me vook ad the shipping. Ve have a Ro Ro vid German BMWs. Id vill go do the Port at Perth Amboy, New Jersey. Ve could pud the 142 vith the BMW shipmend. The dime frame is aboud 10 days."

"What incredible good luck," Hardy said. "What about the availability of two coupes, identical? Could you accommodate that?" The Dutchman paused, surprised by the request. "A minute please. Yes, yes, ve could, sir."

"What about the price for two with shipping?"

"Ve vould request 60,000 guilders for the do dotal."

"With whom am I dealing with please?" Hardy requested.

"I am W-I-M, sir."

"I'll see you late Friday afternoon, Wim, for payment and paperwork. Again, Harden Alden."

"Yes, yes, I vill vait for you. Dank you very much."

Hardy practiced wrapping dollars with saran wrap to his first pair of underpants and putting on a tight second pair to keep it all in place. It would work just fine. He smiled, pleased with his trickiness.

The next Tuesday morning back at the bank, he called an associate, Ed Roget, owner of the GMC dealership in Hartford.

"Ed, Hardy Alden here, I have a favor to ask of you. My cousin here is selling her house and moving back to Wisconsin. She owns a DMC van that is customized for handicap and wants to sell it. I know it's a white elephant for your lot, but it would help her out if you'd take it."

"I guess I don't have a tremendous problem with it," Ed said, agreeing to the request.

"I'm planning on taking her to the Club tonight after work. Would it be possible for you to meet us after six and bring the paperwork for her so it's all set for when she wants to bring the DMC to you? I'll buy."

"I can't say no when you're buying, my friend," Ed said and chuckled.

Hardy clicked the phone again and punched in Cynthia's number. "Hi, Cynthia. I've been busy this morning. Can I pick you up at four-thirty, early, to go to the club? Bring everything you found with you. I'll have a bank bag with me. I'll explain everything then, not on the phone. Things look good."

"Oh, Hardy, thank you. I'll be ready. I love you," Cynthia's voice purred into the phone. She climbed the stairs to the attic with a roll of aluminum foil to secure the guilders.

When Hardy came for her, she handed over to him the tin foil package in the car before they started for the club. He hastily stuffed it into his bank bag and shoved it under his car seat.

At the club he enlightened only the parts to Cynthia that she needed to know.

"I can get the Volvo for you," he concluded. Then he added, "I'm going to be away on business the rest of the week," he said. He did not tell her anything about the Holland plans.

"Hey, there's my friend Ed already. He's early. It's okay. We've talked about everything we needed to already. He must be anxious for a drink." Hardy stood up to shake hands with him. "My cousin, Cynthia Parkton. Ed Roget."

"Nice to meet you," Ed said. "I have everything here in the paperwork for whenever you want to bring your DMC in." The signing of the paperwork transpired right after a drink. With the business with Ed completed, they thanked him and drove back to Cynthia's house. "Oh, Hardy, thank you, thank you," she said as he parked. She gave him a passionate good-night kiss on the cheek. "I just feel so light-headed and jubilant. What a heyday. You've done so much for me again."

He put his arm around and drew her golden head against his chest.

"I'll be the only person in Port Michigan with a car like that Volvo," she murmured to him. She pulled away after giving him a warm second kiss, leaving two red lipstick imprints, and opened the car door to get out.

Amber met her at the door. "You sure look happy tonight, Cynthia," Amber said.

"Yes, yes, I am. The children are already in bed?" she asked Amber, entering the house. Amber nodded, smiling up at her. Cynthia's ecstasy flowed from her. She tucked two dollars into Amber's hand. "Thank you, Amber, thank you. Your father is waiting." She stood hugging herself in the doorway until they pulled away. "A glass of champagne. I'll have a glass of champagne." She walked quietly past the children's rooms. Returning to the kitchen breakfast nook with the champagne, with a chilled glass in her hand she whispered, "I must call Reginald. I need to tell him."

CHAPTER 11

Ashes to Ashes

September 1982, Port Michigan, Wisconsin

"I'm sure lucky you have an apartment for me to rent, Connie," Reginald said. He sat at Connie's kitchen table in Port Michigan, having a drink with her after work. "You know I needed to start working here so I can help Cynthia fix the house she bought. It needs a lot of repair. The job the Blackings invented for me at the cement company is tolerable, but not much pay. More than The Lodge, but I have rent to pay here, not living at Natty's anymore. Oh well, Cynthia is glad I have a job." He rubbed his hands over his nose then lighted a cigarette and took a huge chug of his Meyers and Tab.

"Yes, lucky for you I have an empty apartment," Connie replied, nodding her head in agreement. "So what's up tonight? Going over to Cynthia's again?"

"Yeah, she likes it when I pay attention to Sam."

"Well, he is your son," she said, emphasizing "your son."

"Maybe that does have something to do with it," he said. "She'll have cupboards to mount or otherwise I'll keep working on the electrical wiring tonight. That sure is a neat car she has. She says she doesn't have any money anymore. Just like Natty. Wonder where she came up with the money for that beauty?"

Connie's pug nose wiggled, like a rabbit's, in surprise. Her eagle eyes stared at him. If Reginald couldn't figure that out, it would not be worth the bother to tell him.

September 1982, Hartford, Connecticut

Hardy struggled to raise himself when his hacking cough began again. He lay on the same sofa for two days now. The cough continued to increase in volume with the shaking spasms closer together. The mucus and blood from his nose and mouth on his pink and white pin-striped shirt made it look like toasted paper. The edges of the stripes looked like they were singed by fire from the dried blood. In his coma-like state he knew he needed to go to Cynthia. Heaving a mighty cough he struggled to lower himself to the floor as if overcome with dumb comprehension. Methodically he placed hand in front of hand to struggle a feeble and dazed crawl through the kitchen to the adjoining garage door. Strings of the interior of his lungs swung red from his nose and mouth. Yes, yes, he must make it to Cynthia's side. He prepared for this, his final moment looming, by leaving the driver's door of the Volvo 142 Coupe open, the second car in his garage. Blindly, he pulled himself into the driver's seat next to his beloved Cynthia in the passenger seat to die by her side. His final wretched cough spewed forth a huge heap of nauseous stench. The interior of his lungs forced their way out through his nose, eyes, and mouth. The lung cancer won, like a chalky moonscape in the black night. Blood still dripped from his nose, down the steering wheel, where his body sagged across it. His right arm lay extended to the empty passenger seat.

*****

Amber tried to call her father at the bank every day. He did not answer his private phone. Finally, she contacted her Uncle Mitchell.

"Uncle Mitchell, I walked to Dad's the last two days. He must be working day and night at the bank because he's never home. He's not answering his phone either," Amber said. She sounded anxious and worried.

"Amber, he did not come into work this week yet. It's Wednesday already. Hmmm, it's unusual for him to not at least call and check on a transaction."

"Something must be wrong. Please, please, you need to go to his house right after work to see if he's okay." She started to cry.

Mitchell drove directly to Hardy's house as soon as he could finish at the bank. The white house reflected a deathlike chalk color in the late afternoon sun. Mitchell tried the two doors and even the windows. The interior locks would not give in to his force. He rushed over to the neighbor's house next door to call his wife.

"I think I need to call the police to break in," he said with strained speech.

"Yes, yes, do that, and I'll come right over too. I'll send the kids next door," his wife said.

He hung up, and his trembling voice called the operator to get the police. "Hello, this is Mitchell Alden from the First National Bank. I'm over at my brother Harden's house at 1115 South Vista Road. He didn't come to work this week. His daughter, Amber, who visits him every day says he wasn't at home this week and he didn't answer his phone. The house is locked tight from the inside. We think something is wrong."

"We'll send a squad right over, Mr. Alden."

"Thank you, thank you."

The police arrived in five minutes. They tried the doors and windows.

"Everything locked tight from the inside, sir. We'll need to break in," the police sergeant stated without hesitation to Mitchell. "String the yellow tape," he directed his partner. With the yellow police barrier tape draping the house, they chopped down the door. Nosy neighbors stood rubbernecking. Once inside the stench of death drifted from the open kitchen door and the adjoining garage.

Mitchell stepped backward from the wretched smell to recoup himself.

"Stay outside," he directed his wife who just arrived at the scene. She hurried out quickly to get away.

"The body is in the second car stall," the police sergeant said.

"I didn't know he owned two cars," Mitchell told the police amazed, shaking his head in disbelief. "He bought one like that for our cousin, Cynthia. I can't imagine he owned this, too, identical," he rambled on, stunned, not able to comprehend it. He turned back to the kitchen in fear of vomiting. When the siren of the ambulance wailed in the driveway, the police sergeant drew the overhead garage doors up for the removal of the body. This also revealed the hideous scene to all the gawking neighbors.

*****

The very next day Mitchell met with Judge Whitman in his office.

"So there you have the essence of his will and last wishes. You're the executor of the estate. His request is to have his remains cremated. Your cousin, Cynthia, is to disperse them into the Lake in Wisconsin. You'll need to make the crematory arrangements on this end. By the way, what last name does she go by these days?"

"She went back to her maiden name, Parkton," Mitchell told him.

"I'll send her an official copy of the will and last wishes. He left her thirty thousand dollars. A nice chunk I'd say, but there is plenty more than that for the daughter, Amber, as we both know. That'll be your job as executor, of course, to straighten out all the assets." He lighted a cigar. After thinking a minute, he continued. "The total balance of the estate goes to the daughter. Her college is already provided for according to this. I'll straighten out all the paperwork as quickly as I can."

"Thank you, Judge," Mitchell said. He leaned forward, resting his head on the top of his folded hands on the judge's desk. With a pensive look in his eyes, he stared off a minute. "You know, I don't understand about that second car. I knew he bought one for Cynthia. Why did he have one identical?"

"Maybe his daughter can shed some light on it. I sure don't know. Your first job as executor is to enlighten her with all this information as soon as possible," the judge said with sternness.

"Yes, yes, I know, I'll do that later this afternoon after I take care of the bank. It'll be hard as heck though." He let out a deep sigh. "Thank you for everything. I'll call Cynthia again from work. She is broken up beyond words. Just shocked. She just didn't have a clue about the cancer. The poor, poor dear. Well, none of the rest of us did either. Hardy obviously wanted it that way, always secretive about his personal life." Mitchell wiped the sweat off his palms on his trousers before he and the judge shook hands.

"Anything I can do for the family, don't hesitate. I'll be glad to help out," the judge said.

*****

Mitchell called Amber's home from the bank. Her mother answered on the second ring.

"Hello, Nan, Mitchell here. I met with Judge Whitman already, first thing this morning. Hardy requested me to act as executor of his estate." He paused. With a painful voice he pressed on. "I should meet with Amber as soon as you think she'll be able to comprehend the information."

"Of course, of course, thank you. Amber's here," her mother said. "She couldn't manage school today in any way, shape, or form. I know she'll want to see you. She loved her father so much, Mitchell. Please be as gentle as you can. Whenever you can come is fine."

Mitchell left the bank early to carry through with his duty to meet with them. Amber hugged her tissue box for the next wave of tears waiting for him. When he arrived, Nan opened the front door wide for him.

"Oh, Uncle Mitchell. You're finally here." Amber choked through her tears and hugged him tight. He tried to remain steady during the ordeal. "But no one in our family has ever been cremated," Amber wailed, holding her hands over her face while sobbing on the sofa. "Why does he want Cynthia to throw his ashes into the lake and not me?" She implored an answer from him with her grieving red eyes. He pulled his chair next to her. He took both of her hands and massaged the tops with his thumbs.

"We must do what your dad requested," he whispered to her.

"But why Aunt Cynthia? Why not me?" She began to shake, sobbing violently again.

Nan came to her side to hold her and comfort her. "Darling, I'm going to see Uncle Mitchell to the door. I'll be but a minute." Amber wagged her head up and down indicating an acknowledgment. At the door, "Why, Mitchell, why? Why did he choose Cynthia over his own daughter, who loved him all her waking and sleeping hours? Amber's bedtime prayers always included him." She held back the tears that welled in her eyes. The starriness in her sad eyes begged for an answer. Mitchell had none.

*****

Cynthia, together with Aunt Natty's assistance, made the arrangements for Hardy's memorial service at The Lodge for Saturday, the second weekend of October. Natty knew the priest from the Episcopalian Church in Belmont who would speak. Immediately following his religious reassurance, others would be invited to share their memory of the beloved father, brother, cousin, and friend Harden Alden, if they so desired. After the conclusion of the service, a reception hour would be held in The Lodge with refreshments and hors d' oeuvres. Reginald would be a special guest bartender for the painful event as well as drive his boat, *Temperance*, for the dispersing of Hardy's ashes in the lake. Reginald avoided funerals but kept his boat in the water late in the season this year for the event because Cynthia told him to.

Everyone kept their fingers crossed for a beautiful fall day that Saturday at The Lake. The grand old maple trees displayed their mellow shades of crimson in the soft autumn angled sunlight along the splendid shore. The weeping willow trees cascaded their yellowish brown leaves closer to the ground as they surrendered to the end of autumn. The outside ceremony began late.

"I can't believe Aunt Natty isn't here yet," Cynthia said to Amber. "Me too." Amber raised her teary eyes to meet Cynthia's.

"We need to start, everyone else is here. Let's begin." Cynthia nodded at the clergyman, indicating to him to commence with the service. After his brief remarks about Hardy's chronological life, the hereafter, and God, he invited others to speak. Cynthia spoke of Hardy's wonderful human qualities. She proclaimed her first cousin her faithful friend. Mitchell spoke of Hardy's attributes as a respected businessman and beloved brother. Amber stood weeping in the fading autumn sunlight, gripping the urn. The sunlight shimmering on the water looked like liquid diamonds. In the distance the wail of an ambulance siren and other service vehicles could be heard. They sounded close.

"Come, Amber, you and Uncle Mitchell and I'll go down to Reginald's boat now together. Can you carry the urn okay alone?" Cynthia asked her. "Lucky for us, isn't it, Mitchell, a calm day on the water." Cynthia imagined all the ashes blowing back on her royal blue dress and jacket she selected to wear, a present from Hardy, or worse yet the damn ashes in her face.

The rest of the group meandered into The Lodge for libations. Billy helped out tending bar. When Cynthia returned from sending forth Hardy's ashes into the lake with Amber and Mitchell, she distanced herself from them, sitting stoically at the bar next to Connie.

"I can't believe Natty couldn't keep herself together and sober enough to come down to the memorial. She seemed fine this morning," Cynthia bitched to Billy and Connie.

"Maybe she drank more because she is in mourning," Billy commented sarcastically.

"Let it go, Billy," Connie interjected.

"White wine, Cynthia?" Billy asked, ignoring Connie's comment.

"Can you open a bottle of champagne and keep it out of sight so nobody knows I'm drinking it. I don't want people to think I'm celebrating, you know. I just prefer some champagne right now."

"I can handle your request, my lady," he said and winked at her. "I see Reginald is walking up from putting *Temperance* away now. I'll get you set up before he comes in to take over."

"Thanks, Billy."

"Connie?" Billy questioned.

"Maybe just a red wine, Merlot. I'm leaving soon to drive back to stay with Sammy and Rebecca at Cynthia's in the city tonight. I'll let the babysitter go when I get there. Cynthia and Reginald are staying at Natty's again tonight. Impressive hors d' oeuvres, I won't need to worry about eating tonight. Just feed the kids."

"Mitchell is using estate money to pay for this. Hardy would have wanted an elegant display. I love the shrimp tree," Cynthia said, agreeing.

"What were the sirens for? Anyone know? They sounded close by when I drove *Temperance* over to the dock," Reginald questioned as he shuffled in behind the bar after securing *Temperance* in her slip.

"Sirens? Didn't hear anything in here." Billy shook his head negative, answering him.

The people at the reception exchanged pleasantries mingled with hugs and kisses. After the complementary hour, most guests filtered from the reception. The small group of Mitchell and his wife, Amber and her mother, and Cynthia remained to have dinner together. Mitchell, like Cynthia, chose not to expose his children to the uncustomary cremation service in their family. Mitchell's children remained in Connecticut with friends for the weekend.

"What do you think we should do about Natty?" Cynthia asked. "Try to go upstairs and rouse her for dinner?"

"Oh, let's leave her be," Mitchell said. "We're all stressed out enough from the day."

The five sat quietly at dinner discussing how the service and reception completed the necessary funeral closure. As executive, Mitchell outlined particulars to complete early tomorrow morning with Cynthia before the four of them left to return home to Connecticut.

Two policemen walking into the bar drew the remaining clientele's attention. After one addressed Reginald at the bar, he motioned them toward the table hosting the family.

"Mitchell Alden?" The older policeman with a handlebar mustache questioned.

"Why yes, yes, I am," Mitchell answered, standing up.

"Is Cynthia Parkton here?"

"I'm Cynthia," she managed to say, clearing her throat shocked, wondering what they could want.

"We need to speak to the two of you alone," the officer pressed on.

"But why?" Cynthia blurted out.

"Just outside in the hall, please, miss."

Mitchell steadied her as she stood up. Reginald and Billy watched from the bar.

"What in the hell is happening?" Reginald grumbled to Billy, rubbing his nose vigorously.

"Maybe they're getting arrested for throwing the ashes in the lake. Shit, I don't know." Billy leaned to the right so he could see down the hallway to the foyer better.

*****

"We have learned that Natalie Parkton Crestor is a direct aunt to both of you. She died this afternoon at 2:01 near the corner of Lake Breeze and Spring Grove Roads."

Cynthia collapsed onto the love seat behind her, gripping the arms of it so hard that her white knuckles showed through her tanned fingers.

"She must have decided to walk over to the Johnsons to feed their pets before she came to the service," Cynthia spoke absently. "She is taking care of them for the weekend." Her blue eyes fixed themselves on Mitchell. "Oh, Mitchell, what are we going to do?" she whispered, imploring him to do something.

"The coroner pronounced Natalie Parkton Crestor dead of a massive heart attack." The other policeman droned on. "Now which one of you two is taking charge here?" he questioned.

Cynthia wanted to beat the arms of the love seat, but she felt like her hands were wrapped in gauze.

"Cynthia, you have to." Mitchell squeezed her hand to get her attention. "You're here. At the very least you can drive up here, if need be, to handle affairs. I must be at the bank Monday." He patted her hand now to keep her attention.

"You two can decide, but we need the two of you to come to the safety building together to fill out forms and give information before anyone leaves," the policeman continued.

"Can we do that early tomorrow morning, even though it's Sunday, so I can make my flight out of Port Michigan. Say seven-thirty?" Mitchell asked. "All right with you, Cynthia? I'll bring the papers I need to give you yet in regard to Harden's passing with me."

"Yes, yes, I can."

"Well, it's real unusual, but we'll work it out considering the circumstances. See you in the morning then. Our sympathy goes out to your family. Good night." The two policemen left.

"I'm going to the bar, Mitchell. I can't eat anything more tonight anyway. You can tell your family better without me too. I'll see you in the morning. Thank you." She gave him a brief hug.

"What in hell is going on?" Reginald leaned on the bar, lighting a cigarette as she approached. Billy sat up straight in anticipation of the answer. Cynthia pulled herself up on the barstool next to Billy. She motioned with her hand for Reginald to pour her a wine.

"Natty's dead." Cynthia's mouth opened to let the words out. "She died of a heart attack this afternoon." Her own words surprised her when she spoke them.

"What? You're kidding." Billy took hold of her arm to turn her toward him.

"The sirens, the sirens," Reginald mumbled and mixed together a Meyers and Tab. "That's what the sirens were for. I don't believe it."

"No, no, I'm not kidding." She covered her face with her hands, resting her elbows on the bar. "I can't take any more today," she whispered, shaking her blonde hair. "Billy, will you tend bar for Reginald so we can go upstairs? I need to go up."

"Sure, sure. I'll call Patty first, so she knows this is all on the up-and-up when I don't show up as expected."

Upstairs in Natty's apartment, the two calmed down. Reginald sat down at the round oak table, lighted a cigarette, and took a chug of his fresh Meyers and Tab. "Needs more ice," he said. "What now?"

"It's a good thing I came two days early to clean. It stunk in here. I made Natty put those cats out in the fish house. She didn't like it. I need to call Connie to tell her and see how the kids are. I think I'll have to ask her about tomorrow night, staying again, and probably Monday. You can say good night to Sammy too." He smoked his cigarette. She continued almost talking to herself. "I guess I'm going to be in charge. Mitchell has to leave early tomorrow morning. We must meet at the safety building tomorrow morning already at seven-thirty, so they all can make their fight from Port Michigan. There's paperwork involved, I guess. I'll have to plan what I am wearing tonight. Well, if I'm in charge, I'm having her cremated. It's cheapest. She can be the second in the family," she said. "Reginald, you know, I'm pretty sure Natty has a law firm in Florida she used. We need to look for papers to find the name of it. She always sits at that ancient kitchen table to do her daily business and bills. Rifle through that pile on that table, Reginald." Cynthia shook her head and smiled. "She always did call it piling, not filing. She has that giant rolltop desk in her bedroom. I'll start there. Maybe I'll find my great grandmother's jewels there, too," she said. She smiled wistfully.

"Do you really think we should?" Reginald asked, rubbing his chin and nose.

"Yes, yes, we need to. Especially because it looks like I'll be appointed with the power of attorney over this mess. If there is a law firm, we need the name right away for Monday morning. Let's get going."

At first Reginald found only bills to pay. He could not believe it when he saw a balance of over $5,000 in her everyday checkbook in the pile. He started to rush to the bedroom to tell Cynthia this revelation. She met him hurrying out of Natty's bedroom waving the papers in her hand at Reginald's face.

"I've got the name of that Miami law firm here. I found it."

CHAPTER 12

Terminado Einde

Tuesday, Port Michigan

Reginald chose to drive back to Port Michigan Sunday to be at the cement company on time Monday morning. Tuesday he drove straight to Cynthia's after he finished work.

"Hi," Cynthia said, opening the kitchen door to the driveway. They kissed. Cynthia stepped back from Reginald. "Why don't you take a shower and then I'll tell you everything I finished up before I came home today. The last couple days took a lot of concentration to accomplish what I did before turning it over to the Miami attorneys. I'm tired. Thanks for staying with the kids last night. It gave Connie a break. I just couldn't get back."

"Sure, okay," he said. "Guess I'm pretty filthy. There should still be a change of clothes for me here."

"The kids will be home soon now after school. But that's okay. They'll go outside to play. It's gorgeous out today for October. You know I'm thinking about homeschooling them. I'd really like to. Rebecca is twelve, and Sammy is five and a half now. A perfect time to start for both of them, Rebecca before junior high and Sammy before first grade. Hurry up. Get cleaned up. I've got lots to tell you," she said. She did not want to be near him wearing those appalling work clothes.

Reginald returned to the kitchen table after his shower carrying an ashtray. Samuel and Rebecca already played outside with friends.

"So," she began sitting down at the table. "Want a drink? Pour me a Chardonnay, too, before you sit down."

He fetched the libations and sat down, pulling the ashtray into the correct position beside his Meyers and Tab. He lighted a cigarette.

"Thanks," she said. "After Sunday morning at the courthouse and the final meeting with Mitchell before he left, I went directly over to Jack Sawyer's house so he could draw up the papers to give me power of attorney over Natty's estate. You remember him, don't you? Next to your dad, he's been everybody's family attorney at the lake since day one. He'd sit and drink with Natty on her porch and play with her dog. Well, he knew about Natty already. Small town, news travels fast. There were no issues. He said he could hurry up getting the death certificate first thing Monday morning at the courthouse and that I should meet him at the coroner's office at eleven. He was glad to help. I can't believe Natty's dead. Can you?"

"Nope." He rubbed his nose. "The Blackings were sure surprised by the news when I told them Monday morning at work. I've seen Mary Blacking smashed with Natty on her porch and the two of those old babes lying on the floor trying to do exercises. Not a pretty sight, but they were drinking buddies," he said.

"Anyway during my power of attorney episode, I paid the bills in her pile, and some other things fast. Where that $5,495 came from in that checkbook is beyond me, but it's not there now, and I closed the account. I paid a little visit to the bank first thing this morning before I left and waved my power of attorney paper in there so they wouldn't question my signing the checks that would be coming in," Cynthia said. "Then I went back to Natty's and called the Miami Law firm. They are taking over and are arranging with Jack to have the power of attorney transferred to them immediately—period. They are handling the cremation arrangements and paying for it. Don't ask me why. I'm sure there's no money. We'll have a little memorial service for her next summer. The weird thing is that the law firm wanted your current address and telephone. They said they still showed you living at Natty's. They even wanted to know where you worked. I can't imagine why, can you?"

"Beats me," Reginald said. He rubbed his nose and mouth nervously and got up to mix another cocktail. "I sure don't have any money to pay for her cremation."

"Pour me another wine, too, please. Then I'll call the kids in," she said.

The following morning at his work, a telegram arrived, priority for Mr. Reginald Haley. He ripped it open to read.

Mr. Haley,

The Law Firm of Shriver and Sons SC represents the estate of Natalie Parkton Crestor. Come to our firm in Miami, Florida, ASAP in regard to the estate and reading of the will of the deceased. Call at your FIRST convenience. Collect. We will provide all travel arrangements and expenses.

Sincerely yours,
Steven Shriver, Attorney at Law, Esq.
Shriver and Sons SC
111 Brickell Avenue
Miami, Florida USA
308 748 1928

As soon as his break time came at ten, he called Cynthia to read it to her and ask her what to do.

"For heaven's sake, call them," she said. "At the very least it sounds like a free trip to Florida. You can't beat that."

Nervously, Reginald called the number after asking permission from Mike Blacking.

"Shriver, and Sons, Attorneys at Law," the receptionist answered in a Cuban accent.

"My name is Reginald Haley. I received a telegram to call Steven Shriver," he said, uneasy about the whole situation.

"One moment please, Mr. Haley." Music played for a full minute while he waited on hold.

"Ah, Mr. Haley. Steven Shriver here," Attorney Shriver answered the phone.

"Received your telegram," Reginald cautiously said.

"Yes, yes. On the behalf of the firm, may I offer our sincere sympathy in Miss Crestor's sudden passing. We handled Miss Crestor's divorce and all her affairs since then. Sadly, now we will be administrating her estate. We need for you to fly here tomorrow to commence with the estate settlement and reading of her will," Shriver said.

"Fly there tomorrow?" Reginald said, dumfounded.

"Yes, tomorrow. It's important to read the will immediately because of the nature of her holdings. Then we can progress with legalities," Shriver said.

"But I'm not a relative," Reginald said in protest.

"Never mind that. Miss Crestor specifically named you for hearing the reading of her last will and testament. Can you call us back in a couple of hours? We'll have your travel itinerary for you then," Shriver said.

"I guess so. It'll be my lunch break then," Reginald said.

"Good. We'll wait for your call. You make your arrangements to take off work tomorrow and Friday too."

He immediately called Cynthia to tell her before he told the Blackings he needed to take off work.

"For heaven's sake, go. A free trip to Florida just to sit and listen to Natty's will for a half hour. I wish they'd called me," she said. "Take a book to read, like I always do. You'll need something to read in your Florida downtime," she said and giggled.

At his lunch break, Reginald made the Florida call.

"Yes. Mr. Haley," the receptionist with the Cuban accent answered again. "I have your whole itinerary completed. All you need to do is go to your Port Michigan Airport for the 7:05 morning flight to Miami on American Airlines. Your ticket will be issued to you there. A representative from our firm will be at the Miami International Airport for your arrival here. Oh my. It looks like

Attorney Shriver will be meeting you in person," she said. "How unusual," she added. "A page from our firm will be waiting at your arrival gate holding a sign with your name. Do you have any questions, Mr. Haley?'

"No, nope, I don't know, I don't think so," Reginald said, but he had questions about the whole damn thing.

*****

Reginald's flight landed on time, at 9:17 a.m., at the Miami International Airport. Upon entering the airport, he immediately spotted the young page in a crisp uniform with the law firm's name embroidered on it. He made his way to the fellow holding up a sign with his name.

"I'm Reginald Haley," he said.

"Welcome, Mr. Haley. I'm Page Johnson from our firm. Attorney Shriver is waiting in his limousine. We'll collect your luggage and then go to join him as quickly as possible."

"Sure. I only have one suitcase," Reginald said and shuffled along beside him. After claiming the one worn suitcase, they ascended in the elevator to the parking level. An hour had passed since the page descended the elevator to welcome Reginald at his arrival gate. Now he returned with Reginald in tow. Approaching the vehicle, Reginald could see Attorney Shriver sitting in the rear seat of the law firm's black Cadillac Sedan De Ville limousine scrutinizing papers in his leather briefcase. Quite the car, Reginald thought. The page opened the rear door for Attorney Shriver. Reginald paused slightly behind the page and watched Shriver stand up out of the back seat. He briefly thought it funny that Shriver wore Edmond Allen wing tip shoes. Reginald thought of his father who had worn the same shoes, made in Port Washington. Shriver wore them to remind himself of his Wisconsin roots and his law school days at the University of Wisconsin. Shriver extended his hand.

"Steven Shriver," he said. "Have a good flight?"

"Sure. I've never flown in first class before. Good food." The two men shook hands.

"Over here, please," the dark-skinned driver said, indicating for Reginald to come to the door he held open on the opposite side of the limousine. The page carefully placed Reginald's suitcase remains in the trunk.

"Well, seeing it's almost lunchtime, I've made reservations for us at the Miami Yacht Club. Natty Crestor told me about your interest in yachting." Cleverly, he brought Natty's name into the circumstances immediately.

"We do some sailing up at The Lake in the summer. I'm sure it's nothing compared to what you have here. I sail sometimes, but mostly I'm on the Race Committee," Reginald said. He looked around the luxury Cadillac he rode in and thought, *If the boys at the cement company could only see me now.*

The Miami Yacht Club impressed Reginald beyond any presumption. "I own a Swan 46 Sloop myself," Shriver said. "Moor it right here at the club. I'll show it to you this weekend. My wife named it *Speedy Lady*. Miss Crestor, Natty, sailed with us many times. My wife and she enjoyed Pinot Grigio together. Can't believe Natty's gone." He paused. "Quite a gal. It sure surprised me when her niece called. This afternoon we must get to the office to begin with the paperwork in regard to her passing, right after lunch."

"What paperwork?" Reginald asked. "And this weekend? I need to be back at the cement company Monday, or I won't have a job."

"I'll explain everything as soon as we finish lunch here and are back at the firm. Mind if I call you Reginald? And please, just call me Steve."

"Sure, fine," Reginald said.

After lunch at the law office of Shriver and Sons SC, Reginald found it hard to relax in the wingback brown leather chair.

Shriver began reading out loud. The will commenced in the usual way.

I, Natalie Parkton Crestor, being of sound mind, on this day, the Twenty-fifth Day of July, Nineteen Hundred and Eighty, proclaim this document to be my Last Will and Testament.

Boy, will I be glad when this is over with so I can get out of here,
Reginald thought while Shriver continued reading.

Then the will reading changed from the usual as Steve began to
interpret it to Reginald.

"This means that Miss Crestor named you as sole heir to her
entire estate," Shriver said, "with the minor exception she included
for provisions of her dog, Susan Sunshine, and her cats. You will
officially inherit and assume ownership of her properties at The Lake
and her condominium in South Beach, Florida, as soon as we can
complete and file the paperwork. Every detail will be accurate."

Reginald did not understand. "It'll save you a lot of money if you
change your residency to Florida, the South Beach Condominium.
You'll need to get a Florida driver's license Monday. The other thing
you need is a Florida bank account. We'll have that set up for you
tomorrow. Wisconsin will tax the dickens out of you. That's why
Natty always kept her Florida residency. I know. I'm from Wisconsin.
I graduated from law school at the University of Wisconsin. Probably
that's the reason she solicited our firm to handle her divorce originally," Steve said.

"So did my father. But still I'm not a relative," Reginald said,
confused. He ran his hand over his nose. "Mind if I smoke?"

"No, of course not. Relative or not, Miss Crestor named you to
be her heir, period. Now on to the next part. The Crestor oil wells
and the refineries in Alaska and Long Beach, California, yielded Miss
Crestor an average $500,000 quarterly, depending on the dividend
value. This should explain to you the urgency in settling her will, as
the oil just keeps on flowing out of the wells. She chose not to use
the money for anything but to buy more stock. All private. I think
she wanted to obtain over half ownership and drive the ex-husband
crazy, but that's only my opinion. Our firm's handling fee is 12 percent, $62,500 quarterly, again, depending. We'd continue to hold to
the same disbursement from you, without raising, in solicitation of
your continuing on with us, Reginald."

"I don't understand any of this," Reginald answered. "All I know
is if Natty trusted you, I do too."

"Thank you. Good. Let's shake hands on it today. Make it a gentleman's agreement, the old-fashioned way. All the documents will be ready for signing in the morning," Shriver said. He stood up and extended his arm across his shining mahogany desk for Reginald to shake hands. Reginald leaned forward from the leather chair and shook it. He seemed to be more at ease now in the luxurious chair. The idea of calling the attorney Steve became more comfortable too. Steve punched a button to summon the woman with the Cuban accent to get started on documents immediately.

"You're going to have to stay here into next week. I've made the arrangements for your accommodations at the Fontainebleu," Steve said. "Ben, the owner, is a friend of mine. He lives over in the Mutiny in Coconut Grove. A happening place. Maybe we'll get invited to a party before you fly back."

"But you still don't understand. I really need to be back at my job Monday," Reginald stammered.

"Try to comprehend this, Reginald," Steve continued patiently with him as if he were talking to a child. "You are a reasonably rich man now. You probably won't want to work, and definitely do not need your job at the cement company anymore. I think we'll wind this up for today. I'll notify the driver to be ready to take you to the Fontainebleu, a fabulous hotel. The place for you to buy yourself new clothes and shoes is in the Bal Harbor Shops. The top-drawer men's stores in the United States have their auxiliary shops right there in the Fountainebleu. Just sign your name," Steve said. "You'll want new clothes. Buy three or four changes to start. All you need to do is sign your name. You'll need shoes too. Feel at home. Bask in the sunshine."

Reginald looked down at the beat-up pair of boat shoes he wore.

"Eat at the restaurant, drink at the bars, just sign the tabs. Use room service if you want," Steve said.

"Do you mean you're buying?" Reginald asked, ill at ease again.

"No, you are. Now what time should our driver come for you in the morning? The earlier we get started, the better," Steve said.

"I'm used to being at work at six in the morning."

"Let's say eight," Steve said.

The driver delivered Reginald to the Fountainebleu.

"Follow me, sir." A waiting bellhop grabbed Reginald's shabby suitcase from his hand to carry to the open-air reception arena. At the reception counter Reginald signed the registration forms. The well-groomed female receptionist handed the attending bellhop the room key in the Chateau Versailles Ocean View. Reginald looked around in awe at the luxurious lobby. The spectacular blue waterfall in the center drew his amazed attention.

"This way, sir. Only one suitcase?" the small, short bellhop asked.

"Ah, yeah. That's all," Reginald said, shuffling along beside him in his weather-beaten boat shoes.

"All the shops are this floor. There's a restaurant and cocktail lounge on this floor. Suit and tie. On the top floor, 16, there is a casual dining area and bar. Fashionable resort wear is acceptable there. One of the three swimming pools, a Jacuzzi, and saunas are also on the sixteenth floor."

They stopped at the elevator area. The bellhop pushed the up button. Inside he pushed 3. The door opened to the hallingsworth green stucco hallway. Reginald tramped behind him on the feathery pastel flowered carpeting down one suite to 321.

"Your suite, sir," he said. He unlocked the door open and pushed it open for Reginald to enter first. The attentive bellhop followed him in. He set the suitcase secured by a belt, down by the closet door. Then he drew the aluminum blind to one side. "Your balcony, sir."

Amazed by the view of the Atlantic Ocean, Reginald just stood still and gazed out at it. He took a cigarette from his pack to smoke. The bellhop quickly lighted it. The swaying tops of the Royal Palms brushed his balcony. Beyond them the great Atlantic lapped the endless white sand of Miami Beach.

"Anything else, sir?" the bellhop asked, looking at him quizzically.

"Yeah, can I get a Meyers and Tab?"

"One or two, sir?"

Reginald, surprised, ran his hand over his nose. "Well, two if I can."

"Of course, sir." He walked to the telephone to call room service. "They'll be delivered within five minutes," he said. The bellhop stood waiting. "If everything is okay, sir, I'll leave now," he said.

"Thanks, sure, go ahead," Reginald said.

The bellhop left without a tip. A room service waiter promptly delivered the two Meyers and Tab. Reginald hastily signed the bill. It worked. Excited, he lighted a cigarette. *Well, I'm buying some new clothes. Steve Shriver told me to*, he thought. Reginald hastily chugged his cocktails. Then he strolled down the hallway to the elevator, basking in every sinking footprint on the luxurious carpeting. The elevator car door opened. He passed inside and pushed L.

In the Bal Harbor Shops Courtyard, a young man, suave and dark-haired, approached Reginald immediately.

"Good afternoon, sir. My name is Harold. I will be your personal valet while you are visiting the Bal Harbor Shops Courtyard," he said.

He paid no mind to Reginald's disheveled appearance. He had serviced eccentric millionaires and billionaires before. "What would be your pleasure today, sir? I speak English, French, and Spanish. Please? Shirts, trousers, jackets, shoes?"

"Yeah," Reginald said, trying to remain aloof. "All three, and some shoes too. Boat shoes. Where I come from we talk American."

"Certainly, sir. We'll start with premium Hawaiian shirts with choices by designers, Ted Lapadis, Armani, and Polo, plus countless others. Ah, the beau monde. Would you afford me the honor of guiding you in selecting, sir?"

Reginald nodded his head up and down in agreement. "Two shirts, I want two," he said. Harold wrote with a stroke of his pen and snapped his fingers, summoning gofers to gather the floral tucked shirt attires. He could assess the correct size just glancing at Reginald. "After shirt selections, we will summon complementary trousers. There is a new designer gaining notoriety by the name of Calvin Klein."

"I need two pairs of new jeans, thirty-four by thirty-two, three new polo shirts with a pocket, and two new pairs of boat shoes. I like both Seebago and Docksides," Reginald said.

"Certainly, sir," the valet said, gesturing toward a comfortable gentleman's sitting arena. "Please, sit down. Various men's apparel choices will be here momentarily. Cigarette, sir?"

"Sure," Reginald said.

The valet produced a pack of Benson and Hedges. Reginald frowned, thinking of them as girlie cigarettes, but he took one anyway. He knew they were expensive, plus free. The valet lighted it with a gold-plated lighter. Then Harold made some quick notes in his zippered leather billfold size notebook. Two attendants wheeled a clothing rack, laden with an array of designer names, in front of Reginald. One schlep immediately dropped to the floor to remove Reginald's old shoes. The new boat shoe selection came first with a pair of sandals to wear with no socks, bon ton.

"All those clothes are for me?" Reginald said, motioning toward the rack. He expelled smoke and bit down on the inside of his lower lip.

"Yes, for you to view for your trousseau. Jeffry will assist you in the gentleman's garment quarters." Harold motioned toward the approaching Jeffry wearing a premium Hawaiian shirt and strutting in tailored Calvin Klein linen trousers with turned-up cuffs. He donned a raw silk sport jacket with two rear vents. "His Panama sunshade is the second best fino fino," Harold said, rocking back on the heels of his sandals with pride, observing the look of Jeffrey's total ensemble created by his own miraculous hands.

"Where I come from we want warm clothes to wear this time of year," Reginald said. He frowned at the thought of this Jeffry guy helping him change clothes.

"In Miami, sir, the people are preparing for the yachting season. The tourists that come here from the north in winter only will purchase the new styles, de facto," Harold answered.

"I'd like to try a few things on in my room, and I'll return what I don't want," Reginald said. "It's number 321."

"Yes, sir. If you prefer not to have Jeffry assist you. We will collect your rejected clothing garments at your convenience."

"And how do I order two more Meyers and Tab for my room, a pack of Benson and Hedges, and a hamburger with Swiss cheese and fries?" The more expensive cigarettes appealed to Reginald all of a sudden.

"We'll take care of that for you, sir," Harold said, nodding his head at one attendant.

Reginald returned to 321 to find a full bottle of Meyers waiting for him with Tab, plus a cartoon of Benson and Hedges. A knock on the door announced the arrival of the rolling rack of designer clothes. The next knock delivered the hamburger.

"Put it on the balcony table," Reginald said about the hamburger.

*****

At eight o'clock exactly the following morning, Reginald's room phone rang.

"Your driver is here, Mr. Haley," a clerk from the reception announced.

"Okay, thanks," Reginald said. He had been up since before six smoking cigarettes, waiting, and paging through the yachting magazine he brought along at Cynthia's recommendation.

After arriving at the law office, the finalization of the estate paperwork had been transferred to the conference room instead of Steve Shriver's private office.

"Coffee, Mr. Haley?" a young blonde female page asked.

"No, just ice water. I drink it all day, and an ash tray, please."

"Good morning, Reginald," Steve said, entering the black walnut wood-paneled room. "Everything okay at the Fountainebleu? Looks like you found your way to the men's shops."

"Yeah, morning." Reginald wanted to get the show on the road.

"Nice new jeans, boat shoes, and polo shirt. I have a barber you'd like," Steve commented.

"A barber?" Reginald said and ran his hand over his grown backneck hair.

"We'll set that up later. Right now, let's set to work, commencing the transfer of the oil stock ownership first, continuing on to property in Florida, and ending up with The Lake. All personal property is noted as being part of the locations and will not be itemized, including jewels and jewelry, as you are the sole heir. By the way, the attorney handling this at The Lake is Sawyer. He is also in charge of the provisions for the pets."

"Jewels and jewelry? I didn't ever see Natty wearing any." Reginald shook his head negatively.

"Oh yes, considerable, between family heirlooms and gifts from Jeffry Crestor. Some pretty big rocks. She had all of her gems registered and appraised by quality and carat. We'll get to them next week. I recall that her collection is worth around five million dollars. I'll have all the exact figures with descriptions ready for you Monday."

Reginald sat silent. He rubbed his nose.

"I don't know what I did to deserve all this. I only helped Natty out when I could, played with her cats and dog, and drank a few cocktails with her. Funny thing, I always thought she had some money somewhere, but nothing like this. It wasn't my business anyway. Lucky me, I guess," Reginald nervously said, shaking a Bens and Hedges out of the box.

"Natty always spoke of you with respect. She genuinely liked you. That she named you as her sole heir doesn't surprise me, especially after meeting you. You seem like a pretty decent sort," Steve said.

After signing the papers, a catered lunch arrived to the conference room. Reginald met John and Horace Shriver, the two sons of Steve in the law firm. He thought them all to be honest and smart, like his own father when he had practiced law.

After the lunch, Steve pushed forward. "Signing this bank form will complete all the preludial documents for filing. Unfortunately, it's already three o'clock in the afternoon. Too late today. It'll have to be Monday." He nodded at his son, Horace, assigning him the task. "Long day, Reginald. But we've completed Natty's wishes now with all the estate stock documents transferred. The refinery stock absolutely had to be first. Oil just keeps on gushing, doesn't it. Monday we will progress with the real estate. How about the MYC for cocktails and dinner this evening? You can meet my wife," Steve said. "I can have you picked up at about, shall we say six?"

"Sure, sure, that would be great. You know, I'm a believer now about all this," Reginald said. "It's sinking in." He rubbed nose and reached to light a cigarette. He held it in his hand and continued talking. "I was looking in my yachting magazine I brought along. There's a Grand Banks forty-two made by American Marine of Hong Kong," Reginald said, hesitating. "I could really buy something like that now. Couldn't I?"

"Yes, yes, you could," Steve answered. "I have a friend with a yacht brokers' license. He could handle it for you. You do have the money now."

"I have a girlfriend," Reginald pressed on dreamily. "It's Cynthia, Natty's niece. The one who called you. She's the mother of my son too. I've asked her to marry me. It seems like forever. She never would because I didn't have money." His voice trailed off. "Back to the yacht. There's one in Costa Mesa, California. The Pacific side is where I'd want to be, to go down to El Pleamar. Yeah, that's where we'll go. Cynthia's paradise. She can homeschool the kids. Just like she's always talking about," Reginald said. He paused. "Cynthia said she could get into the Acapulco Yacht Club with her membership card from our yacht club at The Lake. Reciprocal agreement it's called," Reginald continued, almost talking to himself. "We can moor there and live on the yacht for the winter and at The Lake in the summer."

"Hmm, interesting," Steve said, breaking in. "I'm familiar with the place. Herrera from a Latin law firm here in Miami belongs to the Acapulco Yacht Club. Expensive. I could document the yacht for you, if you're serious."

"Serious? Yeah, I'm serious. Cynthia will marry me now," Reginald exclaimed ecstatically, sitting back in his chair. Then he leaned forward. "She'll marry me," he said to Steve, hardly audible. Tears moistened his eyes. *The love of my life will finally marry me now because I have money*, he thought. He rubbed out the cigarette he had just lighted.

"Can I use your telephone, Steve?" he asked.

"Certainly, of course," Steve said, sliding the phone across the table over to him.

"I must call Cynthia. I need to tell her."

ABOUT THE AUTHOR

 Linda Thorndike is an accomplished artist and published, award-winning photographer holding an MFA in photography and Cinema.

She frolicked summers at a historic, romantic lake community in central Wisconsin. She has tapped her keen observation skills to recapture the essence of the heady days of lake living from the 1950s to 1980s in her novel Splendid Shore.

Linda and her husband reside at the lake seasonally now. She loves to study history and is combining this passion with writing historical romance fiction.

Please visit Linda at www.lindathorndikewriter.com.

CPSIA information can be obtained
at www.ICGtesting.com
Printed in the USA
FSHW021954270620

9 781646 282685